MARY
MAUDE
McINTYRE

M. Susan Thuillard

authorHOUSE®

AuthorHouse™
1663 Liberty Drive
Bloomington, IN 47403
www.authorhouse.com
Phone: 833-262-8899

This is a work of fiction. All of the characters, names, incidents, organizations, and dialogue
in this novel are either the products of the author's imagination or are used fictitiously.

Published by AuthorHouse 07/26/2021

ISBN: 978-1-6655-3312-6 (sc)
ISBN: 978-1-6655-3311-9 (e)

CHAPTER ONE

"Mary Maude McIntyre," breathed Ellen as she looked lovingly at her newborn child. "Did you ever see a more perfect girl, or hear a more melodious name?"

Jesse McIntyre, older than Ellen by ten years, looked at his wife of sixteen years and nodded with a slight smile. He loved how her auburn hair fell over her shoulders and covered the baby with softness. He knew how soft that hair was. It was such a contrast to his own black hair. "If that's what you want to name her, My Love, then Mary Maude it will be."

Ellen sighed deeply. After seven miscarriages and stillborn deaths, she had finally produced the perfect child. She knew her husband had hoped for a boy to carry on the family name, but secretly she was glad to have a girl. She pushed aside the images of one little boy who cried and cried, the one she wrapped in a blanket to keep him quiet. Jesse had grieved so about the poor little, blue boy. But, Ellen was relieved that the black-haired boy was gone. And now, she had a perfect princess. She laid a hand against the soft curly red-tinted hair and drifted off to sleep. But, not for long because Mary Maude had her own desires and for now it was to eat.

"Slow down, you greedy little girl," her mother sighed softly as the child gulped the offered repast. Soon Mary Maude slept, but only for three hours. And so it was, she needed to nurse every three hours and there was nothing to do but feed her.

"She may look like an angel," her father commented one day, "but she wails like a demon and demands your attention both day and night."

"We have a child, Jesse," his wife reminded him in her wistful and contented way. "We finally have a child and whatever she wants she will have."

Jesse looked at his wife with in dismay. "Surely you don't intend to give into every whim of one child…" he began.

"She is destined for greatness," his wife replied. "We must hire someone to watch over her."

Jesse frowned. "You mean like a nanny? We already have a nursemaid. Truly, My Dear, I do not make the kind of money to hire a household full of servants."

She smiled sweetly at him. "Then you must make more. Surely you do not want your one and only perfect daughter to be deprived of all she deserves."

"Ellen, you are her mother and you shall take care of her." He stared in amazement as not only his wife looked at him with malevolence, but the tiny girl in her arms mirrored the image of her mother. *Why, she's only a few weeks old,* he thought. *How can she look so fierce?*

"I have a good job, Ellen, but I do not intend to work myself to death so you can play out some kind of princess fantasy with the child. I am her father and the husband of this household and we will raise her with common sense, not this tolerance you are dreaming of."

"Jesse, how can you talk so mean to us?" Ellen asked with a pretty pout. "If you would just hold her for awhile, you would soon change your mind about how precious she is." She held the baby out for her husband to take.

"It is no use giving the girl to me, Ellen. She doesn't like me and I do not want to listen to her squalling." With these words, he walked toward the door. "I shall be home late again this evening," he said as the door shut firmly behind him.

Ellen sighed, half in contentment and half in relief. "Papa has changed so," she murmured to her child. "He never used to be so mean." Mary Maude looked up adoringly at her mother then closed her eyes in restful slumber. "See," Ellen whispered. "The perfect little angel."

And indulge her, she did. She hired help from the poor folks across the tracks, those who would work for practically nothing, but to have free room and board and food in their bellies. However, when they showed any kind of initiative with her child, like teaching her new words or to read, she fired them and went hunting another young replacement.

Jesse was appalled at the attachment his wife had with this child. It was as though she had forgotten all about their older girl, like she had replaced her with this new one. He thought about his oldest daughter, Katie Jean, disabled as she was, not able to walk or get around on her own, mute and sad. She was a beautiful child with near-black hair, streaked with auburn locks. She had a beautiful smile, but she sat most days in her wheelchair, needing nursing attention for her many allergies and illnesses. His wife had doted on her ill child, too, after she was born. But, when she showed signs of disability, Ellen lost interest. As years went on, his wife left more and more work to the constant stream of nurses caring for the child's various needs. Then came the years of miscarriages and tragedies to their offspring, a still-born boy and two more who died silently in the night when they were only days old, and another girl who only lived a few months, all with Jesse's ebony locks, all beautiful to Jesse. However, after Mary Maude was born, Mary Maude with her red locks and green eyes, Ellen literally never went into Katie Jean's room again. She was totally devoted to this baby.

Mary Maude ate on a schedule far different from Jesse and Ellen. It was as though there were always meals being prepared. Ellen insisted that Mary Maude had numerous allergies and that textures bothered the child. She had the nanny fix food at least six times a day. Katie Jean ate her customary meals through a feeding tube and was never allowed to join them at the dinner table on a regular basis. Jesse ate breakfast with the nurse in the kitchen, then went to work. He had his lunch with a friend from work and took a late supper with his wife in the spacious dining room at home.

Jesse always spent an hour with Katie Jean, reading to her and taking care of her needs after the nanny left for the night. He often held her hand and talked about the world and the things Katie Jean wasn't able to see outside. Sometimes, Jesse would take her out onto the patio and point out flowers and trees, small animals and birds. Katie Jean seemed to enjoy their time together and Jesse got a certain satisfaction from the interludes as well. "I wish I could make life less difficult for you," he said softly.

Katie Jean smiled in her disarming way. She was quite a beautiful girl even though she was so weak and ill.

"I love you, My Dear," Jesse said to her every day without fail.

As Mary Maude got older, she became bitter and whiney. Jesse had no say in how she was raised, so he mostly stayed out of the way. He gave in to his wife's desire for a nanny and brought them home one after another because they were "never good enough." He found some of the poorer class from town who lived down near the railway, and who would accept less money, but he always told them it would be hard work and they wouldn't be employed for long. He knew his wife and daughter and their picky ways.

Mary Maude would complain sweetly about yet another young nanny and in silent glee would watch as Father drove each one away in his car. She was always happy to greet a new one, would play games and show them all around their neighborhood, especially to the botanical garden her father kept, where they could walk and talk. But she would soon tire of the new nanny and begin finding things to complain about. Especially if they wanted her to do studies or learn music or to sew. And another one would have go away. Mary Maude would watch from behind the sheer curtains of her bedroom suite in the grand old Victorian home where they lived. Papa would help the girl into the car and away they would go. "Where does he take them?" She wondered aloud. She began imagining her father driving to some dark alley amid winding, poorly-lit streets in a city and shoving the girl out onto the street... Or, maybe he would take them to the railroad and shove them onto a train to go far, far away... And, then again, he might take them to the country and shove them out on a back road, making them walk home, wherever home was for the girls that came to them. "I don't care," she declared! "I just want them gone, dead, or whatever. They're tiresome girls."

In reality, they didn't live anywhere near a city, just a small, country town along the railway, and yet there was a 'poorer side' to the citizenry with their segregation of classes.

Jesse hated the business of taking the girls home, back to a poverty-stricken household where there were generally too many mouths to feed and not nearly enough food or money. He knew the little stipend he offered didn't give much relief, but now there would be nothing for them, again. He always told them how sorry he was that they couldn't stay, that he couldn't help them more. Most girls just shrugged his comments away as they glumly got out of the car on one of the many winding streets on the north side of town. He tried to never think of them again, of the sad faces and the struggle for them not to cry. He could almost cry himself, but for the fact he had to act like an adult, even if he didn't feel much like one on those dreary days. He would then drive back to the south edge of town where his wife's secluded home sat along a rutted side road which needed repair. "Like the house," Jesse would sigh. "There is always work to do and never enough time to do it."

That all changed with Andrea. Andrea was in her twenties, dark skinned, with shining black hair. She was a nursemaid to her own mother, and she lasted a little longer with Mary Maude than some of the others. She was not a beauty as to looks, but she had a sweet spirit that appealed to everyone, especially Jesse. She didn't live in the house, rather he picked her up each day and dropped her off again at her home each evening. They spent some time together when Jesse volunteered to help her with maintenance in their home. He wasn't very good at the job, but the time spent with Andrea and her ailing mother was a joy to him. He marveled at how much time he could find to be available for his handyman chores at Andrea's home while his own house became more and more neglected. Somehow, he found the time to go walking in the park with Andrea on her day off from her duties. Then, they also found time to spend together gardening in the small plot she cultivated behind her house. She was well-read and Jesse loved to listen to her recite a new poem or phrase from something she had just finished. Some of this he passed on to Katie Jean when he found time to spend with his older daughter. Most of all, Andrea made him laugh. He realized he hadn't laughed in years. Life at home was so dreary with one invalid child and another that seemed to loathe him. His wife, Ellen, barely paid any attention to him at all. He had quit going to her bedchamber soon after Mary Maude came to live with them.

And that is how he thought of the child, that she had come to live with them, not that she had been born to them. Jesse also felt somewhat guilty at not being able to spend more time with Katie Jean. Yet he watched in silent joy as Andrea taught Katie Jean to read, to draw, and to sew a fine seam. It gave him pleasure to watch Katie Jean emulate Andrea, laugh often, and become a young woman of some beauty. She looked more like her mother than Mary Maude did, he realized with renewed wonder. *Perhaps her beautiful auburn hair has saved her,* he thought. Then he shook the thought away as unworthy. *What am I thinking, that Ellen somehow put a curse on each one with dark hair, but allowed the two red-heads to live? That's preposterous! How can I entertain such thoughts/* He turned his attention to Katie Jean and took pride and joy in what she was learning, realizing she was growing more than ever before. She excelled in her studies and quickly picked up mathematics. She had become animated, talking to him at length when he tucked her into bed at night. He began to hope she would have a life of her own someday. He never realized that she could learn, that if he had put more effort into her, or if Ellen had, Katie Jean could grow up quite normally, albeit in her wheelchair.

At last, Mary Maude got tired of even Andrea. But, Jesse didn't. He didn't bring her back to the house, but he did spend every free moment with her, continuing her pay long after she was no longer coming to work for them. He also began to feel a love for her that he couldn't explain. Eventually, they became intimately involved and Jesse longed to have a life with Andrea; dreamed of it, in fact. He also felt guilty about Ellen and how he betrayed her, but not guilty enough to give up the secret love he enjoyed.

*   *   *   *   *

As Mary Maude became a teen, her demands were even more outrageous. She no longer had a nanny, but now had a daily teacher. Again, the long line of teachers began to mount up. If Mary Maude became restless, she would insist on no lessons, but to have walks in the park or to go horseback riding. Jesse had to admit, the girl was an excellent rider. However, she was not excellent at schoolwork. Some teachers quit outright, but many had to be let go because Mary Maude was simply tired of them and their routine of studies. He never knew what really happened to one named Nancy. She had been a frail young woman, pale with blonde, thin hair and faded blue eyes, but she was stubborn and willing to attempt teaching Mary Maude. He came home late one evening to find her dead by the fireplace, in his parlor. "What on earth happened?" He asked his wife and their daughter.

"We don't know," Ellen insisted. "She must have fallen down the staircase, I suppose. She was lying dead at the bottom of the stairs and I moved her in here."

Mary Maude smiled in a way that made his blood curdle. She nodded her head, almost happily, at her mother's story.

"Did you not call for Dr. Brown?" He asked.

"No need," his wife replied. "She had no family or anyone who cares. Perhaps we can just bury her ourselves out in the garden."

"Of course we can't do anything of the kind!" He blustered. "Whatever are you thinking?"

"I'm thinking of our daughter. If it is known that a teacher died here in our service, we'll never get another decent person to come in." She paused. "I already had to care for the other child myself today because I didn't want some nosy nurse coming in and finding our problem." She pointed at the dead girl. Placing her hand on his arm and smiling up sweetly at him she added. "Please for me, Dear. Just take her out into the garden and bury her. No one will ever know. These girls come and go, you know. We'll say she left and that will be the truth of the matter."

Jesse shook his head, but finally gave in and placed the limp body in a wheelbarrow he got out of the barn. He got a shovel and a blanket, then began his grizzly task. He walked around the beautiful garden, with its shrubs and flowers and finally settled on the rose garden. Under a large yellow rose bush, he began digging a hole. When he had it shaped like he wanted, he got out the tractor to dig it deep. Jesse spent some time washing off the bucket of the tractor, before he placed the blanket inside and laid the body gently upon it. He drove slowly to the hole near the bush of yellow roses. He groaned as he got off the tractor and bent down to smell the sweet flowers. Jesse laid Nancy next to the hole and jumped down into it. He then gently brought the body into the hole and laid her across his feet. He covered her as best he could with the blanket before pulling himself out of the hole, then filling in the hole once again. He had dirt left over which he spread under the rose bushes nearby. That task done, he once again washed the tractor and himself with a hose at the pump, before he went into the house and showered for a very long time.

For the first time in over ten years, his wife came to him in the night. After she left for her own bedchamber, Jesse paced the floor in worry and doubt. His dreams, when he finally did lie down to sleep, were tormented by the face of the young woman, Nancy. He longed to see Andrea, but suddenly feared for her safety if ever Ellen or Mary Maude were to find out about his trysts with the wonderful young woman. He also wondered if she would ever want to see him again, if she were to know what he had just done. "No, I mustn't ever see her again. I must protect her above all else."

Before going to work the next day, Jesse again showered, then went out to check the roses, making sure the girl had not come up out of the ground. He vomited on the grave, scraping some dirt over it with his shoe. He walked into his garage where he wiped the shoe off with a rag. "I must see Andrea," he whispered. "I cannot bear this alone." The promise he made to himself the night before faded in the light of day.

Jesse went to Andrea's home before work where he was met at the door by a stranger who proclaimed that Andrea's mother had died in the night and that Andrea was not at home. Jesse had never seen the fellow before, but assumed he was her brother who had left home years ago, the one who helped her support herself in the house. The young man resembled Andrea, with the same set to his jaw and dark eyes. Jesse left his name, and as he walked away, he felt that he had lost everything good in life because of the deed he'd done. He worked languidly at his job and returned home at night weighed down with his sorrow after a quick stop at the liquor store for a bottle of Southern Comfort to help him sleep. It became his pattern, a hopeless existence of work and drunken sleep.

Another nurse or maid or teacher, he wasn't sure anymore, evidently died in her sleep. Jesse was just expected to dispose of this body, too. He wasn't hiring the girls now, his wife and Mary Maude had taken over that duty. But, this was too much to bear. What was he going to do? It was becoming a pattern that he no longer took the girls home, but planted them like so many rose bushes in the garden. How many had there been now? Three, five? He didn't know. During the summer, he had a building put up out at the far end of the woods, beyond the garden and orchard. He called it the Sugar Shack and pretended he was going to make maple syrup out there. He even spent time researching how to make syrup and entertained the thought that he really would build a stove and make some syrup. But, of course, he didn't do it. There was just the furnace / operating room and a storage room. Now, he could cremate the bodies and spread the ashes over the flower garden as fertilizer.

Jesse cringed at work when his co-workers tried to talk to him about anything, really. He didn't know what to say. Truthfully, he was afraid to talk in case he blurted out what was happening in his home. He wondered again about his own children who had died. *Surely Ellen has not… No, it was too horrible to think about. He loved her. They had a life together and he was sure she couldn't ever… But, am I sure? Why did the boys die? What about the little girl with black hair? Only the one with her own red hair had survived, and Katie Jean.* Jesse began drinking more often to "take the edge off and have normal conversations with others."

When he came home one evening, he was greeted by a woman he'd never seen before. "I'm the new teacher and maid," she announced proudly. Indeed, she was dressed like a French maid, but with a long skirt. Her brown hair was pulled back into a tight bun which didn't do her justice.

Jesse pushed his way past her to the dining room where he found his family gathered at the table. Even Katie Jean was propped up at the table. "What is this?" He asked weakly.

"We decided to celebrate Katie Jean's birthday!" Mary Maude announced. "We're having a party!"

"Her birthday?" He questioned. "This isn't…"

His wife waved away his protest. "Never mind," Ellen said. "We're celebrating because we somehow missed it earlier. So bad of me, but we're happy now, aren't we, Dear?" She patted Katie Jean's hand.

Indeed, there sat his oldest daughter in one of the captain's chairs at the table, propped by pillows and surrounded by gifts. She looked adoringly at her mother, enjoying the attention she had missed for most of her short life. In front of her there was a cake decorated with candles.

"Is there no supper?" Jesse asked.

"Oh, we ate early so we could have this party," Mary Maude said with a bright smile.

That girl is up to something, he thought of Mary Maude as a shudder passed over him. *I don't want to think about what it could be. That Girl. Now I think of my own daughter as That Girl.* Jesse shook his head slowly to clear the dark thoughts.

"I'll get your plate from the oven," the new teacher-maid smiled as she disappeared into the kitchen.

"What are we paying her?" He asked of his wife.

"The usual, I suppose," she answered.

Jesse wiped his forehead, thinking of the money that was going out and how he could continue to pay both a nurse and another teacher. "I don't see how," he commented realizing the nurse was not at the party. "Where's Katie Jean's nurse?" He asked.

"We gave her the night off. This is just a night for family," Mary Maude announced.

"And the new teacher," he mumbled.

His wife waved away his concern. "Really Dear, she is both a teacher and a maid." She and Mary Maude began singing the birthday song as the teacher-maid came back with a steaming plate of food. Jesse could barely eat.

It felt as though they sang languidly, the sound of it ringing in Jesse's ears as he tried to choke down some food. He looked up and realized that Katie Jean was smiling and clapping. This celebration was pleasing to her. Taking heart at the sight, he pushed his plate aside and joined in the fun of giving her gifts. They were thoughtful items of clothing and toiletries that she would be able to use. He smiled weakly at his wife. *If I can just push away the thoughts of those poor girls out in the garden,* he thought weakly. *And of Andrea. I suppose I can stop paying her to make up the difference in what will now be paid to this new teacher-maid.* The thought of Andrea caused tears to form and they dripped down his face before he even noticed them.

When Katie Jean became tired, Jesse carried her up the stairs where he administered her nightly medicines, putting her safely into her bed. He smiled into her trusting eyes, trying to read what her thoughts might be. "I love you, My Dear," he whispered with a kiss to her cheek.

It's all right, Father," she whispered back. "I barely need a nurse anymore. I'm quite capable of caring for myself." She gave her crooked smile as she closed her eyes.

Jesse marveled again at how much his daughter had advanced. He never dreamed she would ever talk, let alone care for herself.

The happiness was short-lived, of course. Sometime in the night, Katie Jean had evidently tried to come back downstairs in her wheelchair, although why was never made clear. In all her life, she never brought her chair near the stairs, except to park it in the hallway so someone could carry her down the stairs. Most of the time she spent in her own suite of rooms with a nanny or a nurse, or a teacher. Ellen, Jesse's wife, evidently, had tried to stop her, but they both had tumbled down the steep steps. That is, Ellen tumbled over and over with the chair while Katie Jean held onto a post of the banister, halting herself. She had only a nasty gash on the back of her head, some minor bruises and a laceration to her leg. Mary Maude had witnessed the whole thing, weeping and reporting it to her father. Jesse studied his daughter in the dim light of the parlor while they waited for the coroner and the police to arrive. He listened as sirens came closer to the home. Mary Maude sat reading a book as though nothing had happened. Her teacher sat near her, crying silently into a handkerchief, her face pale and frightened.

Truly, the next few days were a blur for Jesse. Mary Maude seemed to take over all the arrangements and made all the decisions. He felt as though he had floated through the days and was in a stupor at night. *What could have happened? How could both of them have fallen down the stairs?* He shuddered as he thought of his wife and daughter tumbling down the steep stairwell with the wheelchair. *Why would Katie Jean ever have gone so near the stairs in her chair? She had never been one to sleepwalk, yet it all happened just the same.* "Yet neither of them ever cried out Mary Maude said," he mumbled to himself. He pictured himself being awakened by the sound of the chair bumping its way down the steps, hitting the banister and the wall. He was sure he had heard a startled cry, although Mary Maude denied it.

Katie Jean's injuries healed rapidly while his wife suffered a broken neck and back. She also had a gash to the back of her head, a deep wound that could have been caused by one of the leg braces of the wheelchair. Jesse had run out into the hallway to see Mary Maude standing at the top of the stairs, a look of . . . "What was that look? Horror? Fear? Surely not satisfaction," Jesse shook his head as he held it in his hands. Jesse remembered the blood on the stairs, but what concerned him was the blood at the top of the stairs. Mary Maude had "tried to clean up," but there were still traces of blood. "I can't think about it," Jesse whispered as he drowned his sorrow in yet another bottle of whiskey.

He found himself in that position again, sitting on the patio in a lawn chair, holding his head in his hands. He looked up at the garden before him. Mary Maude had insisted that her mother be buried in the garden, "So I can sit out there with her every day," she whimpered. "I miss her so." And so it was, that Jesse made arrangements for a burial in the garden, a proper burial approved by the state board of health and the community. He put a marker on the grave, just a simple flat stone with a plaque on it, barely visible if you weren't looking for it there near the white roses, across the garden from the yellow ones. Jesse didn't want anyone to know what was beneath those beautiful yellow flowers, yet he himself, could barely look away from them. They seemed more beautiful than ever. *Fertilized by the remains of those poor girls,* he thought.

Jesse shuddered at the thought of the half-smile on his daughter's face during the tragedy, the blood on the stairs. Mary Maude often looked at him as though he were a bug or some ugly thing from under a rock. He realized that he was fearful of his own daughter, unsure of her moods and motives. At nineteen, he felt she was some kind of monster. He believed she had killed her mother and tried to kill her sister, but he couldn't prove it. He was unsure if his own wife had helped her kill the maids or if Mary Maude had done it all. He broke out in a sweat just thinking that dear Ellen could have had something to do with those deaths, yet he felt deep within himself that she was at the root of the evil, that she had taught her daughter this evil. He knew he had to remove Katie Jean from the home before something more tragic happened to her, too.

Over the following weeks, Jesse made arrangements for his eldest daughter, now into her twenties, to live in a home for young ladies in a city some distance away. *I will visit her when I can,* he thought. And he did visit every few weeks. Katie Jean told him stories of times Mary Maude had come to her room and stared at her sleeping form. When Katie Jean awoke, she felt fear that her sister was just standing there, staring. "I didn't know what to do about it, Father."

Jesse had no answers for her. He didn't know what to do about Mary Maude, either. He felt a cold panic that she might kill Katie Jean next, but getting his daughter into a home was taking more time than he thought it would. He tried to calm her by reminding her that she was now safe and didn't have to worry about what her sister might do once she was safely moved into her new home.

"But you still live out there, Father. Are you in danger from her?"

"No, no, My Dear, don't think like that," he would protest. However, he also wondered about what his daughter would do, what she thought about, and how it would affect them all. He didn't have to tell Katie Jean that there had been other nursemaids who had died in their home one way or another. Talking about that would just upset Katie Jean more, he was sure. *We're a family of secret-keepers,* he thought. *We don't tell and we don't ask. I don't even know what Katie Jean knows about it all, herself. I don't think I'm in any danger, they just get rid of girls or women they don't want around anymore.* A shudder shook him. *Or defenseless babies.* Tears coursed down his face.

Jesse continued his visits to his daughter more for his own comfort than for hers. She had projects and went out into the community as she told him each week, but in time, there became less and less for them to talk about. Guilt overcame his natural goodness and Jesse fell into despair.

In a lucid moment, Jesse thought of his life and what had happened to his family. *And now my wife is buried out there in the garden, only yards away from those poor girls who also fell down the stairs or died in their beds,* he thought. *And there will just be more and more, it seems..* He shuddered as he thought of yet another new maid in the house right now. *How long does she have?* His body shook heavily as he took yet another drink of the whiskey that was helping him calm his thoughts and feelings. He had not gone to work for a whole week, he thought. He looked down at himself and realized he also had not showered or changed his clothes. His face felt fuzzy with unshaved whiskers as he rubbed his hand over his cheeks. "This isn't like me," he whispered. "But, what kind of person have I become? I've allowed my own daughter to kill. I'm sure she has, just as her mother before her." A shiver of fear coursed over him. "How can I ever go back to work? I couldn't face anyone with this knowledge. They must all think I'm the monster." He drank himself into yet another stupor. It didn't occur to him that his old friends had gone on with their lives and scarcely remembered him. They almost certainly did not know what he was doing or how he and his daughter were living in the old homestead. While he thought that he had missed only a week of work, it had been months since he had left the house and there was no more job, even if he went back to the office. Jesse had lost complete track of time.

Over a few months, the old home also fell into its own kind of despair and disrepair just as Jesse declined. Jesse never fully recovered from the incident. He managed to attend Katie Jean's marriage to a young man who seemed very well connected, but she refused to come to the farm again, moving away with her husband. Jesse was never to know his grandchildren, but Katie Jean did write to him when her son and then a daughter were born. "At least something good came from our marriage, Ellen," he whispered to the sky. "Our oldest, disabled daughter was more of a person than the whole girl you doted upon and spoiled into this strange creature." He shuddered at his whispered words.

As years melted away into more years, Jesse became a shadow of his former self. He sold the horses and sold off some acreage to pay bills. His daughter acted out some fantasy of her own, in the old home. She hired a young man from town as a caretaker, giving him room and board for his labor. Jesse noticed he really didn't do much, but he did keep the major repairs done up and mowed the lawn out front. The back yard was overgrown and had become Jesse's haven out of the house. Mary Maude ran everything else.

One day, Mary Maude came to him out in the porch which he had converted into a bedroom for himself. "Papa, what are these old papers?" She was waving sheets of paper in his face.

"Hold them still so I can see," he complained.

Mary Maude shoved them into his hands. Jesse tried not to shake as he smoothed out the papers and read them. Somewhere in the back of his mind, he held a memory. "Why these are about your mother's family," he almost whispered. "There's a trust, I believe," he wiped at his watery eyes to see better. "Yes, I remember that Ellen's grandfather left her a trust and this old farm…"

"What's that mean to me?" Mary Maude wheedled. "Well, I mean to us, Father; is there money to be had?"

Jesse hated the sinister tone of her voice and the honey in her words. He nodded. "Yes, Child," he replied. "I'd forgotten this old trust. We never tapped into it in all those years of need." Jesse shook his head. "I used to have a good job, you know."

"I'll call the bank," Mary Maude said as she grabbed the papers from him.

"No, no!" He got up from his chair with effort. "It doesn't work that way. We'll need to call Pastor Williams. He's the attorney who handled the estate way back when."

"Okay, I'll call him, then," Mary Maude sped away from him.

"Daughter!" Jesse croaked in what he thought was a shout. "I must do this. The estate is mine, not yours. He won't talk to you about this."

Mary Maude turned on Jesse with a look of hatred in her eyes.

Jesse stopped moving toward her. "He won't talk to you," he repeated.

"Well, hurry up then and call him," she demanded holding out the receiver to the phone as Jesse made his way into the hallway.

Jesse sighed as he brushed past her to the desk and found the book where Ellen kept phone numbers. He found what he wanted and dialed the number. Mary Maude stood beside him. Of course, it wasn't an easy task. First of all, the number was an old one, no longer in service. Then, they discovered that the attorney had died years before. In the end, Jesse made an appointment to go to the new office and see one of their estate attorneys. The trust was registered with the state and was in the records at the court, so it was still viable. The appointment was two weeks away.

Mary Maude was disappointed, yet pleased too, that they had found this source of income for the home. She began making plans to fix up the house and have some landscaping done. Jesse had to remind her that they didn't know how much was in the trust or if they could even access it. "I'll clean up and go back to work," he explained.

"Where?" She scoffed. "You drank that all away years ago."

"Years?" Jesse questioned. He looked confused. "How many years?"

"I don't know, five maybe," she barked back at him. "You've been drunk ever since Mama died."

Jesse couldn't believe it had been that long. He went to his room upstairs and was appalled to see the dust and disorder in his bedchamber. Through tears of pain and frustration, he began putting things away. He busied himself for the rest of the day and well into the night, cleaning and organizing. When he had the room like he wanted it, he closed the door. Then he went to work on his wife's room which was in just as much disarray as his had been. Ellen would have been so disappointed, he knew. He wondered why Mary Maude had let these rooms go. Again, he finished and closed the door, walking downstairs never to return to those rooms again. He fell upon his dirty cot and slept for twenty-eight hours, straight.

Jesse walked out to the crematory in the old orchard which he called the Sugar Shack, once pretending that he would make syrup out there in the furnace, he remembered. He had gathered tools for butchering and the necessary medical items needed to tend to bodies. It was all in fairly good repair, just a little dusty. He didn't go out there too often. He had the old barn rebuilt and began to keep hogs, actual animals he could butcher so he could keep food on the table. It gave him an odd sense of pride to think he was providing for his family in some small way.

As he began to sober up, he looked through the old desk and found his ledger where he used to keep up with the bills. In the back of it were papers he'd kept that had been from his own family. This farm had been Ellen's, but he might have a little money of his own if he was smart enough to track it down. He called his friend at the bank and got help to apply for an annuity that had been left by his grandparents, and he was astonished at the amount that had grown in it, and he was also relieved that he would be able to keep the household going just with that. He didn't need Ellen's money or the farm. He built fantasies about moving away, getting a place near Katie Jean or something. But, of course he didn't do any of it. He was worn down and ashamed of himself and feared his daughter's wrath.

And then, there was the trust left not to him, but to Mary Maude, of course. He had never known that Ellen had changed her will. He never thought of it after her death. There was sufficient insurance with which he paid the bills and went on with his sordid life. Now, it seemed, there was money flowing in from everywhere. He bought another case of whiskey.

Jesse left the hiring of housemaids to his daughter. He hired some of the homeless to help him with the farm chores, but they had a habit of running off when they got a few good meals into them and what little money Jesse could spare. There was one, Jesse shuddered at the memory. He was the one who fell from the barn roof and impaled himself on a fence post. It was a grizzly sight and horrific as Jesse cut him down and cremated the remains.

The current teacher-maid lasted longer than most as far as house-help went, but she too, died in her sleep in the bed assigned to her. Jesse cremated her body and spread her ashes in his rose garden where he had spread those of the hired hand, and others.

Jesse began to take some pride in the rose garden. The yellow roses were growing so beautifully. He pruned them and smiled at the thought of the remains of those who were fertilizing the flowers. He expected Mary Maude would produce more fertilizer for him, so he expanded the area for the roses and transplanted some cuttings to produce an even greater area of lovely flowers and shrubs. In the center was the grave of his wife surrounded by white roses, the only white roses in the growing array of blooms.

Even his general hired help on the farm came and went, much like the girls. When they didn't work out or Jesse tired of them, he followed his daughter's pattern and found them space in his garden. They were lost souls most of them, anyway. They had no one in the world and relied on others for their keep. He burned their meager belongings along with the bodies. No sense in leaving behind anything that would identify them as being on the farm. Any identifiable items left from the fire, Jesse buried deep in the woods.

Jesse touched his roses softly and sighed. *How had it all come to this? I'm not God, after all. And, I'm not a monster........ am I?* Jesse shook his head, his shaggy hair brushing against his face. He pulled at his beard and wondered again how life had gotten him in this predicament. A stray wind stirred and the flowers bobbed for his attention. A slight smile crossed his face. "Yes, you are lovely, aren't you?" He lightly stroked the flowers, trailing his hand over the varied bushes. "Ouch!" Jesse yelped as his fingers brushed over a thorn. He stuck his finger into his mouth and sucked off the blood. He noticed a few drops on a yellow petal and a sudden chill passed over him at the realization of his humanness and the lives he had seen ended at this place. He looked up at the old house, its appearance looking haggard and run-down. He knew the front of the home was in good shape, but the back was deplorable. "Like my life," he whispered to the wind. A single tear wound its way down his dusty cheek before dripping from his hairy chin. With another sigh and slight shudder, he turned his thoughts to Sam, the new hired man; someone he was beginning to rely on, someone who was willing to build two benches to be placed in the garden where he could sit and admire his flowers as he rested from his labors, or sleep in a drunken stupor in the heat of the summer. Sam was nearly Jesse's age, Jesse thought. *Well, maybe he's ten years younger, I guess.* Still, he was strong and not as unkempt as some others who Jesse had hired. Sam had a high forehead, his hair thinning on top. His hair was brown with gray streaks. Sam had twinkling, brown eyes. He liked to make a joke when he and Jesse were alone, but mostly, Sam was quiet, especially around Mary Maude.

Jesse realized that he knew some of the names for those who were nourishing his flowers. He softly repeated their names as he looked at specific flowers where their remains rested in the soil. "Nancy, the first; Sally, Maria, Nancy, Delila, Thomas, Bernard, and of course, Ellen." His gaze fell onto the white roses with his smile.

There were eight more cremations over the following ten years, five from the house and three from the farm. Jesse barely knew who they were, now, just that their ashes were fertilizing his flowers. He spent his days in the garden, took his meals on the patio or in the kitchen, and slept in what had once been the pantry, a part of the porch, now converted into a barren bedroom with only a single bed, a small dresser, and a chair. It was enough for him. "It's all I deserve," he said as he surveyed his room. He had cleaned it up some, but it still bore the semblance of a jail cell.

Sometime in all those years, Mary Maude and Sam were married. Sam was so honored to be chosen by "such a lady," as the mistress of the grand house where he worked. He had been living on the streets for a few years, scrabbling for food and fighting over a coveted doorway for shelter at night. When Jesse approached him, and chose him to work for him, he could hardly believe his luck! He didn't mind that Mary Maude was odd and aloof. She still gave him his own bedroom in the house and three meals every day. And he didn't have to work too hard, either.

Sam stayed to himself and did as he was told. There was quite a bit of repair work to be done on the house, but mostly he worked outside, taking breaks whenever he wanted, never having a time clock or to be accountable for much of what he did. He built benches, repaired the barn and the front of the house, realizing that it was important to Mary Maude for the home to look like it was still nice, at least from the front.

Sam stayed away from Jesse at first, viewing him as crazy. "Kind of like other homeless people I know." But, after a time, he began helping the older man with his garden and realized that Jesse was just quiet and drank too much. He tried joking with him when they were alone, but Jesse didn't respond or act like he appreciated it, so Sam quit. Together, they cremated the bodies of each young woman who died in the house, just like they did the pig carcasses. Sam never asked unnecessary questions, just accepted that there were a lot of accidents and deaths in the sad, old house. He did ask about the tools in the sugar shack and found places for all of them. "What you do with that big grinder, make sausage?" He asked Jesse one day.

Jesse spluttered and began coughing. When he was done choking, he answered in a hoarse voice. "No, that there is for grinding up anything that doesn't get burned up in the furnace, before we spread it outside, don't you see?"

"Guess I never saw you use it, then." Sam scratched his head.

"There's a grinder in the kitchen and Mary Maude makes sausage sometimes with that." Jesse shook his head. "Don't care much for sausage myself."

"Really? Tastes mighty fine to me, almost as good as bacon or ham. But to each his own," he added quickly as he noticed Jesse beginning to frown.

"Just stick to your job, Sam. You're doin' real good here. I'm glad to have you."

Sam smiled, thinking to himself that the old man had some nerve acting like he owned the place half the time.

One summer day, Mary Maude ordered Sam to shower and dress up in some fancy suit. He laughed out loud at the thought, but Mary Maude was serious, and Sam did as he was told. Surprisingly, the suit fit him well enough. She told him it had been her father's. Sam thought her father, too, must have died and he felt sorry for her because she was so lonely. He truly viewed Jesse as another lost soul working for the sad lady of the house. It surprised him to find out that Jesse was her father. That day, the day he dressed up like a fine gentleman, he became Mary Maude's husband. They all went to a local church and a minister did it up right. It was another shock to find out what her plans had been, for him to marry her! He had to sign with an ex which Jesse witnessed for him. Mary Maude laughed it off like it was nothing important and his love for her began to grow. She accepted him just like he was. He had never thought before that time that he would someday have his own family. He became very fond of his wife and would do anything she asked, no questions asked by him.

CHAPTER TWO

Mary Maude watched from the upstairs window as her husband, Sam, took the body from the barn in a wheelbarrow and trudged toward the woods beyond the corn shed. He paused and looked up at her and she nodded at him in acknowledgement, before he lifted his load of debris and soon disappeared into the trees. "I wonder what he does with them," she mused aloud repeating the words she had asked all those years ago when Jesse had taken the housekeepers, nurses, or teachers away. "Does he have some grand ceremony or a ritual of some kind before he cremates them? They're such tiresome girls. Well, not to worry," she smiled her crooked smile. She knew of the Sugar Shack, of course, but she had no idea what exactly took place there other than it was a furnace, not a boiler for syrup. As she turned from the window, she looked at the closed door across the hallway from her bedroom. There was no noise and it pleased her. Her niece, Carla, must be settling into her room. Maybe this one would be the one to keep forever.

A cell phone rang and Mary Maude frowned. Didn't Carla know that those evil things weren't allowed in this house? Didn't Sam tell her the rules? She heard the murmur of a voice from within the bedroom and rushed to the door to eavesdrop on the conversation.

"Yes, I'm fine. Mary Maude is kind and Sam is kind of funny…No, I won't be calling much…They don't like cell phones so I don't think they want me to use it…No, Mama, she just wants me to stay for the summer, I think…Yeah, I think their maid or helper, whatever she was left or something…Okay…Well, I've gotta go, Mama, there's stuff to do…Bye, love you, too."

Satisfied, Mary Maude decided to let Carla keep the phone for now. It seemed she was going to be a good girl and not be calling people all the time. "Good," she said under her breath as she moved to the head of the stairs. She looked down the steep steps and a memory flashed across her mind. She watched in horror as her dear mother and her sister fell crashing to the bottom with the wheelchair on these very stairs. As the vision cleared, Mary Maude held tightly to the railing and stepped carefully down the stairs. At the bottom, she was careful to avoid stepping on the stained floor where her maid's blood had spilled and colored the wood floor forever. No matter what she did, she could not get the stain to go away. "Mama didn't bleed like that," she muttered. Sam had told her that a rug would cover the stain, but she was afraid that she would step on it without knowing it if the rug covered it up, and she couldn't stand to think about that.

She went into the kitchen to put wood into the old cook stove, stoking it up to get it good and hot. She filled an old kettle at the sink and placed it on the stove. *Sam will want some tea when he comes in*, she thought. She glanced out the window facing the woods and saw a plume of smoke lifting high above the trees.

"Is there a fire in the woods?" Carla asked as she stepped into the kitchen.

"Sam's just burning some trash out in the Sugar Shack," Mary Maude said calmly. "Want some tea?"

Carla smiled at her aunt. "What kind have you got?"

"Just herbal teas. We try to eat and drink healthy."

"Sure, I'll have some."

"Sit yourself down and I'll get it for us." She busied herself for a few moments with the making of the tea. "You know, your mama and I were great friends when we were younger," she ventured, watching for a reaction from the younger woman. "Cinnamon stick?" She held up the brown stick for Carla to grab.

"No thanks, just some sugar."

"Honey's better for you and cinnamon cures diabetes." Mary Maude offered.

"Sugar for me," Carla smiled.

Mary Maude stared at the girl for a moment, realizing Carla looked a lot more like her than she looked like her mother. That pleased her.

"I know mama lived here when grandma was alive, but I didn't know for sure if you were close friends," Carla replied with a slight frown. *I don't think Mama even liked you,* she thought more privately. *She still doesn't.*

21

"Well, I don't 'spose Mama's tell their daughters everything," Mary Maude smiled. "Especially when there's family secrets to keep."

Carla frowned, but kept silent. "This is good tea," she ventured on a new subject. "What kind is it?"

"Just some old weed Sam brings me from the woods once in awhile," Mary Maude answered. "Grows wild down there by the lake, I think." She waved a hand nonchalantly toward the window. "I just call it swamp weed," she laughed. "There's these here cinnamon sticks to dip in it, if you want. Cinnamon's healthy and will keep your body sugars where they're supposed to be." Mary Maude tried once again to persuade her niece.

"There's a lake? Could we go fishing or on a picnic…"

"NO!" Mary Maude swung around, a large knife in her hand.

"O…okay," Carla said meekly.

"I just mean that we don't ever go into them woods. Sam says there's some kind of evil out there, so don't think about going out there, even to the lake. Papa wouldn't ever let us girls go out there." She was thoughtful for a moment. "Not that your Mama could ever go outside to play or anything like that."

"I won't go near it then," Carla said quietly with her head down. *And I won't stay here very long, either,* she thought. *Mom was right, Aunt Em is creepy, if not crazy.*

"It used to be just an orchard out there," Maude said as if to herself. Now it's all grown up into a tangled woods, but Sam does keep some of the orchard part trimmed up right along the edge there. He brings up some apples, pears and cherries sometimes."

Carla tried to appear interested, but if she couldn't go out there, then what was the point? She determined to sneak out to the trees sometime… "The flowers are real pretty out there," Carla waved a hand at the window.

"Yes," Mary Maude said slowly, looking at the window herself. "Sam takes real good care of the roses, just like Papa did."

"Do you have horses, Auntie Em?" Carla asked. "Mama remembered there being horses when she was a girl.

"What?" Mary Maude started as if she just realized she wasn't alone. "Oh, no, Papa sold the horses years ago. Just some pigs and barn cats out there now."

"Oh," Carla was disappointed. "I was hoping to be able to ride."

"I used to ride when I was a girl." Mary Maude said thoughtfully. "I don't know why I quit because I quite enjoyed it. We went to competitions and everything. Somewhere in this old house are some trophies I won at the fair and for jumping."

"Really?" Carla was impressed. "I didn't know you did all that."

"Your Mama only told you what she wanted you to hear, I expect," Mary Maude nodded sagely. "I won state championships and everything." Mary Maude bragged to her niece. "Of course, your Mama couldn't ride like me."

"No, I suppose not," Carla agreed. *I already know she won some special Olympics for her riding. I also know you didn't win as much as you're remembering.* "Ever do barrels?" She asked innocently. "I have a couple of friends who do barrel racing at the fair where we live."

Mary Maude looked at her niece with suspicion. *What does she think she knows?* She wondered. "Yeah, I rode barrels for a season or two. Took a bad fall and had to give it up."

And that was the end of horses for both of you, Carla thought. *Once you were hurt, your mother made you both quit riding and got rid of your horses. It wasn't all your father's fault. Wow, memories are tricky things.*

*   *   *   *   *

Later in the day, Mary Maude looked wistfully out her bedroom window, something she realized she often did. *Where has life gone to?* She wondered as she looked down at her hands clasped before her. *When did I get old?* She rubbed her hands together, looking up at the blue sky. "I still miss you, Mama," she sighed as memories drifted through her mind like the puffs of clouds sailing on a breeze outside her window. "I needed you more than I thought at the time." She pictured once again how her mother tumbled down the stairs after her sister and the wheelchair. "It was so easy," she whispered as she sighed again. *Why did Mama reach out like that? What was she trying to do? She should have just let the wheelchair go on down the stairs, without her. Maybe Katie Jean would have gone to the bottom instead of Mama.* Another sigh. *But then, I wouldn't have Carla. I hope she stays. She's so much like me and I never got to raise any of my babies.* Flashes of her little boys sleeping in their crib, the pillows handy along the sides.

I didn't keep any boys Mama, she thought, looking up at the ceiling. Just like you, I didn't keep them.

As a little girl, Mary Maude had played in the very yard she could see from the window, right there near the apple trees. Mary Maude admired the trees and the prolific flower garden Sam kept. "Everything he grows is so beautiful," she murmured, admiring the colorful growth of roses, again. "Mama always loved roses…" A slight frown crossed her brow as her vision settled on the roof and smokestack of the old sugar shack at the far edge of the woods beyond the garden. "Papa built that years ago," she sighed out of habit. "I wonder how many…" she shook her head. No use asking questions. "Out of sight, out of mind, Mama always said," she commented.

Her mind drifted to the babies she wasn't able to have. She miscarried over and over again, each time becoming less and less important to her. Two babies actually were born, a set of twin boys, but both of them were blue and Mary Maude ordered Sam to "get rid of that." Instead of doing as she asked, Sam rubbed them and cleaned out their mouths, blowing gently into his son's nostrils and mouth. They both revived. Mary Maude was horrified and glad at the same time. She thought of her baby brothers that her mother said died before she was born. "Boys ain't worth nothing," Mama told her. So, soon after the boys were born, they 'died' in their sleep. Sam was inconsolable at first, but she insisted that he "take care of them." She just wanted them out of the house and out of her sight.

She didn't know what he did with them and she never asked. Now, she wondered if he buried them with her parents or if they were just more ashes spread out over the garden and flowers. "Maybe they're in the orchard," she whispered.

"Auntie Em?" Carla walked up to her aunt.

Mary Maude scowled at the girl. She knew her extended family members called her Em but she had never heard it used to her face until this girl came to live in the house. "What!?" she snarled.

Carla took a step back. "I…uh, I just wondered if I could do anything to help you."

"With what?" Mary Maude's thoughts were still on her lost babies.

"Cleaning, cooking, anything I can do," Carla explained.

Mary Maude stared hard at her niece, noticing for the first time the reddish-blonde highlights in the girl's hair. After a moment, her features softened. "I'm sorry, Carla. You did come here to help me. I've had to do everything myself for so long, I've forgotten my manners." She smiled, revealing large, rather yellow teeth with cavities. A thought of the recent maid still smoldering out in the sugar shack flitted across her mind unbidden.

Carla smiled timidly. "I truly want to be of help."

"Of course you do," Mary Maude boomed in her loud, masculine voice, more in control of herself. "Let's see, we should make a list for us to follow every day. You know, like a chore chart." There was no response, so Mary Maude hurried on. "I'll work on that while you dust mop all these upstairs floors. They sure need it."

Carla looked around at the clean floor before her. She suppressed a sigh before quietly going downstairs to retrieve the dust mop from the janitor's closet off the kitchen. "It's no use arguing with her," Carla muttered under her breath. "If she thinks it needs mopped, then I'll just do it. Shouldn't take long, there's no dust anywhere."

Mary Maude watched as her young niece walked away. "Maybe she really will settle in," she whispered, looking out the window once again. "Maybe she will be my daughter. Maybe she's the one." Memories of her own babies who didn't survive crossed her mind's eye again. *Mama's babies didn't live either, just me and Katie Jean.* Mary Maude thought. *If you can call Katie Jean's crippled existence a life.* Mary Maude shook her head as she whispered to the window. "Mama wasn't the one who was supposed to die." A single tear coursed down her face and along her jawline. "Why did you grab for that old wheelchair?" Mary Maude blew out a breath of air and shook her head to clear her mind. "No use thinking like that," she said. "It's all history anyway."

But her thoughts weren't ready to give up. There were the many housemaids who, one by one, all died. She looked up at the old sugar shack again, out the window and across the grounds. A tendril of white smoke rose gently in the morning air, blending with the clouds high above. Mary Maude frowned in her customary expression. "What else can he be burning now?" she mumbled.

*   *   *   *   *

Sam was showing his new farmhand how to prepare a fire in the old burner. "Use this here knob to make it hotter," he said. "I already checked the fuel tank and it's plumb full. When the gauge says 1000° let me know."

"Whew! What you burning up?" Lester, the new man asked.

"Sam glared at the younger man. "I told you already we have to burn up that old hog carcass!" He growled. He sized up the younger man. *Not that young, really,* he thought. *scruffy, like all the street people. Strong, that's good. He'll work out if he can keep quiet and do his work.*

"Sorry," Lester breathed. He turned up the knob on the furnace then began organizing the accumulation of junk in the shed.

"I want this all spic and span, but don't you put nothing on that there table" Sam stated, pointing to an old metal medical table near the furnace.

Lester looked at the table with its array of medical tools and an assortment of saws, hanging above it on the wall. There was a big restaurant-style double sink, too and a big barrel full of old, dirty rags and other trash. On a bench was a large grinder. "What kind of a place have I got myself into?" he muttered, shaking his head while getting back to the work. He kept an eye on the gauge until it reached 1000°, at which time he went in search of his new employer. He found him in the garden as usual and told him about the furnace.

Lester helped Sam push and pull the wheelbarrow into the shack. It stunk of putrifying meat from a hog butchered sometime before. Together they put the bones and meat scraps into the furnace tray on the rollers that went into the furnace. Sam turned up the heat which rose quickly to over 1500°. "Shove her in," Sam demanded.

Lester had been looking closely at some of the bones. They didn't all appear to be from the hog. "Must've had a big butchering day," Lester commented with a smile as Sam slammed shut the furnace door with a metal bar.

"Shaddup," Sam snarled.

Lester went quickly back to sorting tools and junk, getting ready to power wash the walls and paint them. *Can't lose this job,* he thought. *A tidy room, three squares a day, a new set of duds, and some cash to boot!* He smiled at his own thoughts. "Sure beats a box in an alley somewheres," he muttered.

"Eh?" Sam asked.

Lester was startled. He thought the older man had gone outside. "Oh, nuthin'," he answered. "Just thinkin' I'm glad to have a job, is all."

Sam looked around the room. "You're doin' okay," he said before turning abruptly with the empty wheelbarrow and going out the door. He stopped at the water spigot to rinse out the barrow before stowing it in the barn up by the house.

Mary Maude watched Sam cross the driveway on his way to the barn. "He's getting old," she said. "What'll I do when he's too old? He'll die just like Papa, I guess." She looked thoughtfully toward the sugar shack and its column of thin, white smoke.

*   *   *   *   *

"Got that hog taken care of, finally," Sam said as he came into the kitchen an hour or two later. "A couple hundred pounds of meat is in the freezer."

"Good," Mary Maude answered. "How's that new fella working out?"

Sam scratched his bearded chin. "Not bad so far," he said. "Hard worker; don't have to follow him about."

"That's good, then," she agreed.

"Yep; not nosy neither," they looked pointedly at one another. "Keeps his mouth shut, mostly."

Mary Maude smiled. "That IS good," she said. "Maybe he'll be able to ease some of your burden around the flower beds."

Sam washed his hands at the kitchen sink. "How's the girl?"

"Carla? She's fine so far, just fine."

"They all are in the beginning, aren't they?"

"Yes,' she sighed. "That's true enough, I guess."

"Think she'll stay?"

"It's too early to tell. And there's family involved, too. This isn't some strange girl off the street this time."

"Hmmmmm...Yep," he nodded. "Well, maybe she's the perfect fit then." He smiled at his wife of over twenty years, reaching up to replace an errant lock of her graying hair above her ear.

"Where's Papa?" She asked abruptly.

"What do you mean?" He frowned.

"Where'd you put him when he died?"

Sam nodded. She'd been truly fond of her father although she was tough enough on him and his drinking. "He's out there near the white roses, the last ones he planted. There by your Mama."

"Oh," she answered, looking down at her hands.

Sam watched her for a few seconds before speaking. "Why, Maudie?"

"Oh, I don't know. I just wondered." She answered. "Is he actually near Mama?"

He nodded. "Almost next to, as far as I can tell," Sam said. "That's why he planted those white roses over there, you know, smack dab in the middle of everything. There's an old stone marker with her name on it. I'll scratch his name on there too, if you want."

Her voice fell to a whisper. "And the babies, Sam? Did you put them out there with Mama and Papa, too? Or....." She stopped, suddenly not able to go on.

"I didn't burn our boys, Maudie. I buried them right there next to your Mama, on t'other side from your Papa. I laid a little cross there in the dirt for each of them. Do you want their names on those crosses, then?" Sam was a little astonished at this conversation. Mary Maude had never asked him about the two boys that had been born, two little elves who only lived a few days, then died in the night.

"Okay, then. That's fine, Sam, just fine." She turned away to get him a plate of food and some tea. "There's a fair in town. Shall we go and walk around? Maybe we can get some cotton candy and caramel corn," she suggested, peering around the doorway into the dining room where he went to sit, while she prepared his food.

"Hmpf," he answered, already looking at the newspaper.

"Maybe Lester and Carla would like to go. Do you think that's a good idea, or is it too soon?"

"I dunno," he replied. "They ain't been here that long, you know."

"Papa loved to go to the fair," she said wistfully, putting Sam's food in front of him. "And Carla isn't a local, so the only worry would be Lester, right? Let's go. I really want to go."

Sam looked at her. "What's all this worry about Jesse all of a sudden?" he asked.

"I don't know," she pondered. "Yesterday was his birthday…"

"Ahhh," he said as he took a bite. "James and Harold," he said between bites.

"What?" She looked truly perplexed.

"I named the boys James and Harold Barnes. Me and you never talked of it, but I called them that, just the same."

Mary Maude stared at him for several seconds. "James and Harold," she muttered. My grandfather was named James. Did you know that?"

Sam nodded, wiping his mouth with his napkin. "Yeah, I did. And Harold was my daddy's name, too."

Mary Maude nodded. "Well, I guess that's that, then."

"They're done up all proper with little boxes I built and everything," he said with a little pride in his words.

"We got another letter from that Donna Sue's mother," she offered to break the awkward silence..

"Oh?"

"She wants her things."

Sam looked up. "What things?"

"Says her daughter had some things with her, a radio and stuff."

"Didn't you tell her the girl run off?"

Mary Maude nodded. "Yes, I did, but she says she doesn't believe it." She paused, "Wants to come out here and get her stuff."

Sam scratched his head before forking the rest of the food into his mouth. "Well, there airn't no stuff that I know of so if she shows up, I guess I'll just send her a-packin'," Sam grinned.

"Says she has her birth certificate." She paused. "Do you know of such a thing?"

"Well, sure, Maudie," he answered. "Everybody has one of those."

"Our babies didn't, Sam," she said quietly. "Papa and Momma didn't as far as I know. I never found anything like that."

Sam stared at her for a moment. "Well, that could be something…." He wiped a hand over his face.

"Will it matter?"

"Don't rightly know. If there's nobody here, then there shouldn't be no certificate, neither, I guess."

"I never thought of certificates. Papa didn't have one for him dying. Did he need one? Do the babies need one, now that we've named them and all?"

Sam was getting irritated. "Too many questions, Maudie!" He barked. "Why think of all this now?"

"That letter got me to thinking we might be in some kind of trouble, Sam," she said quietly. Too quietly for Mary Maude. "Mama had a certificate and everything for her dying."

Sam looked at her. "Well, what do you want me to do about it?" He stood up suddenly, causing the dining room chair to fall backward with a loud bang on the polished wood floor. "Your Papa died right here with us. Nobody knew about him, whether he lived or died, so what difference can it make now?"

Mary Maude looked up at him, towering there over her. "Sit down, Sam, you'll scare the girl."

"Maudie," he said slowly, looking past her. "The Girl ain't in the room."

Mary Maude waved a hand at him indicating his empty chair. "I got this out," she held up a paper. "It's Mama's death certificate, seeing as how she was buried all proper and all, even if it is on our own property."

Sam picked up the chair and sat down. "Okay, so what?"

"Well, we needed it back then because of the will and all." She waved a hand again around the room. "This was her Grand Daddy's farm and he left it to her. When Mama died, she left it to me."

Sam stared at her without talking.

"So, I think we need a certificate about Papa dying to show that I own this place and that his old annuity should come to me." She smiled bleakly. "I think it needs to be all legal-like, you know? Maybe I need to go to the bank and make sure that money is there for me to use, legal-like."

"What's that got to do with the Donna-girl?" Sam removed his old, slouch hat and scratched his greasy hair.

"You need a shower, Sam," Mary Maude said offhandedly.

"Hmpf," He replied.

"Can we make some certificates, copying this one of Mama's or something?"

He frowned. "I don't know how to do something like that, Maudie. I just don't know." He sighed. "Again, what's it got to do with the girl and her stuff?"

Mary Maude sighed in return. "I don't know, Sam. It just got me to thinking about Papa and all. I know he had that old annuity and a bank account, and I've never done anything about it. There might be money to help us run this old place, don't you see?" She looked up at him, but he didn't respond. "I'm going to have Carla help me get a computer and teach me how to use it," she said. "I think we'll need a copy machine or something, too. It might cost quite a bit, I'm not sure." She looked at him with a smile. "I don't know why I've procrastinated this. Papa and I did the same thing when Mama died. We let it go for years when we could have used it all along. I think he and Mama did the same thing, too, when they were pinching pennies all those years until I finally brought it to his attention. I went rummaging through the old desk and there was all the papers. Now, I did the same thing and he had all these papers in the back of his old ledger."

Sam stood up again, grabbing his hat from the table and putting it on his head, readjusting it until he had it just like he wanted it. Shaking his head a bit, he said, "I don't know, Maudie. I just don't know. I suppose you're gonna spend the money no matter what I think." He shook his head, not looking at his wife. "What have we gone and done? Other than your father, if nobody knew these people, a paper just shows we know something about what happened to them, don't 'cha think?" With that, he walked out the door and kept walking, down the driveway, out onto the road, walking away like he'd never come back.

Mary Maude followed him to the door, watching him go. "You'll see, Sam," she whispered. "You'll see."

*   *   *   *   *

Carla was surprised at the question. "You want to buy a laptop?" She asked.

Mary Maude shook her head. "No, Child, I want to buy a computer."

Carla smiled. "Yes, well, a laptop is a computer and is more versatile than a desk computer."

"Well, that's why I'm asking you to help me," Mary Maude said. "I don't know anything about them. Can you teach me?"

"Sure," Carla said. "I'd be glad to teach you. Have you ever used a typewriter?"

"I have one that Mama taught me my schoolwork on when we couldn't get any more teachers," Mary Maude smiled broadly. "I used to pretend I was a great author and typed out some dreadful stories."

"Good," Carla said. "Using a computer is a lot like typing. You'll get the hang of it in no time. Are you going to get the internet, then?"

31

"The internet?"

"Yes, you know so you can go online and look up things."

Mary Maude looked perplexed. "I don't think I'll need that, will I? I mean, we have the phone and all."

Carla laughed out loud, surprisingly sounding a lot like her aunt. "We'll cross that bridge later. But, you might need a printer if you plan on making forms or sending letters or something."

Mary Maude frowned, her voice becoming tense. "Why do you say that?"

"What?" Carla asked in confusion.

"Why do you think I want to make forms?"

"I don't. I mean, well, when people get a computer, they usually get a printer in case they want to print out something. Letters, forms, and pictures are the most common things they print."

Mary Maude shook her head. "Of course, forgive me, I'm just a silly woman, always suspicious of everything."

Carla looked carefully at her aunt. "Mama told me that. About you, I mean."

"Did she?" Mary Maude looked interested. "What else did she say about me? I'm sure she had a lot to say after all these years."

Carla ducked her head. "Well, nothing much, really."

"Don't lie to me, Girl! Don't ever lie to me! That's what I especially hate, the lies and stealing that everyone does."

"I'm sorry. I didn't mean to lie. I also don't want to hurt your feelings or betray my mother in any way."

Mary Maude snorted. "Betray her? She knows all about betrayal, doesn't she? Don't think I haven't heard the stories she's told. If there was ever a liar, it's her! She had our daddy wrapped around her little finger for years! I couldn't have any relationship with him until she left and he stayed with me. So, obviously I was the real favorite!"

"Auntie Em," Carla spread out her hands in desperation. "This is exactly what I don't want to do with you. I don't want in the middle of what ever trouble you and Mama had. I actually like living here and I'm glad I came. I don't want to be your enemy."

"You have no idea what it's like to be my enemy, Carla," Mary Maude suddenly became very quiet. "My enemies don't last long around here," she waved to include the house. "Sam sees to that."

"Sam?" Carla looked confused. "Did Sam take your father's place in that?"

"What do you mean? What do you know of my father?" Mary Maude peered menacingly at Carla, her voice taking on a fierceness, too.

"Only going by what Mama said about growing up here, that her father, and yours, used to take the girls away who didn't work out in your Mama's employ." She paused, but when there was no reaction from her aunt, she continued. "So, I assumed that Sam does that now that your father died. It just made sense to me."

Mary Maude went through a gamut of emotions which showed plainly on her face. With a sigh, she apologized to Carla again. "I'm sorry. I see that I jumped to conclusions again." A rare, genuine smile crossed her lips. "I always expect the worst. Your mother and I didn't get along very well, it's true. I always tell people we did because I don't want their nosy questions. I don't think I can fool you with that one. After Mama died, Papa took Katie Jean away. I never saw her again. She wrote letters to me, but I was angry and didn't answer them. I burned each and every one in the cookstove, right there in the kitchen. I didn't want her to be Papa's favorite, but she always was. Even in his last breath, he called out her name, not mine, and he hadn't seen her in years." She took a huge breath and stopped speaking. Slapping her hands against her legs, she gave a half-hearted bark of a laugh. "Well, I haven't spoken so much in a very long time, especially about my private past. Let's go to town, and you can help me get what I need." She looked keenly at Carla. "A printer, eh? It's not called a copy machine?"

Carla smiled. "Yes, Auntie Em, a printer, a laptop, some ink, and paper. Copy machines are from the dark ages or used in offices where they make hundreds of copies."

They both laughed at that before Mary Maude answered. "Well, that sounds expensive, but if it's what we need, then so be it. I've got some legal business to look into, too. So, it may take us awhile. Get your jacket, it's turned chilly outside."

Carla ran lightly up the stairs to her bedroom. She paused to look at the closet door. "I'm sorry, Ellie, for whatever happened to you. I believe I'm going to have a much better relationship with my aunt than you did." Carla laid a hand on the closet door and sighed, then she grabbed her jacket off the back of the straight wooden chair and hurried down the steps. "A shopping trip!" She said gleefully.

CHAPTER THREE

"Who's Ellie?" Carla asked one morning.

Mary Maude turned from the stove where she was cooking eggs for breakfast. "Ellie or Ellen? Ellen was my mother's name."

"Um… yeah, I mean Ellie," Carla answered as she got out dishes to set the table.

"Why do you ask?"

"Oh, well, I found a scrap of paper with her name on it…"

"Where?!" Mary Maude demanded, cutting her off.

Carla stopped what she was doing, turning to face her aunt. *Auntie Em, Mama calls her. That's not even funny anymore. It's too hard to call her by her name, though. She scares me sometimes and I'm not even sure why. Be careful what you say, just be careful.* "It was in my bedside stand, in the drawer."

"Why were you snooping around?"

"It was in my room, Auntie Em. I put things in that drawer and there it was."

Mary Maud laughed suddenly. "Of course! How foolish of me! I've had so many maids who have stolen from me and snooped around in my stuff… Once again, I'm sorry, Carla."

Carla smiled before resuming her work. "It's okay," she said shyly. *But, what are you hiding that you always think I'm going to do something to find out secrets?*

"Where is this paper?" Mary Maude asked, trying to sound casual.

"I'll go get it. I threw it away, but I'm sure it's still there in my trash." Carla scurried out of the room, practically running up the stairs to her bedroom. Once inside, she closed the door and quickly retrieved the small journal she had found, from her bag. She turned to the last page

34

and carefully tore off the bottom, containing the name. "Sorry, Ellie," she whispered. Carla carefully put the journal in the very back corner of the shelf in the closet, under a box of books. She made sure it couldn't be seen and hurried back to the kitchen with the scrap of paper in her hand. "Here," she handed it to her aunt.

"Took you long enough," Mary Maude grumbled. "This is it?"

Carla looked directly at Mary Maude. "Uh, yeah. Who is it anyway?"

Mary Maude let out a snort. "Just a servant girl we hired awhile back."

"Oh," Carla answered.

Mary Maude threw the paper into the fire in the old cookstove. "No matter," she said.

"Will the new guy be eating with us?" Carla asked instead of asking about Ellie again like she wanted to do.

Mary Maude smiled vaguely. "Yes," she said thoughtfully. "Yes, set him a plate, too."

Dinner was a somber occasion. There was no talking at the table because Mary Maude simply wouldn't allow it. Carla watched them all through downcast eyes. Sam just shoveled his food into his mouth. Mary Maude ate primly, wiping her mouth daintily with a napkin after nearly every bite. Lester, the hired man, seemed to be uncomfortable, looking up at everyone once in awhile like he wanted to say something, but didn't know how to start. Carla smiled at him then looked down at her plate and ate her meal.

When the meal ended, Mary Maude asked Carla to bring out the tea kettle and fill all their cups. "Tell me, Lester," she began. "Did you grow up on a farm? Do you know about plants and animals and such like?"

Lester appeared startled that the conversation was directed at him. "Well, as a lad I spent a fair enough time on my grandpa's old place. Just a gentleman farmer, you know. Kind of like old Sam, here." He nodded at her husband.

Sam looked up from his plate, placing his napkin on the table. "Old Sam?" He asked.

Mary Maude laughed heartily. It was an infectious laugh that caused Carla to almost spill the cups of tea she was pouring.

"Well, we're hardly young, Sam!" Mary Maude stated with another chortle.

"Hmpf," Sam spat out. "He ain't that young neither."

"Well, it's true," Lester said. "Just maybe a tad younger than you, eh?"

Mary Maude laughed again at the frown on Sam's face.

This was the first time Carla had seen laugher and joking in the house. She smiled again at Lester, who grinned back at her.

"So, you seem to know a bit about carpentry and stuff. Did you learn that on your grandpa's farm too?"

Lester frowned into his tea for a few seconds. "No, Ma'am. I had me a few jobs here and there. Just picked up some learnin' about building and stuff."

"Well, that will come in handy around here, won't it Old Sam?" Mary Maude laughed again at the scowl Sam gave her.

Happy as it seemed at the time, of course, it was short-lived. They drank their tea and the men went outside. Mary Maude said she had a headache and disappeared to her room. Carla was left to clean up the dining room and the kitchen. "Well, that's what you're here for, right?" She said to herself. "You wanted to help and get to know her and here you are."

That evening, Mary Maude suggested a game of Clue. Carla was again surprised to know her aunt kept some board games in her own room, on a shelf in the closet. Lester had to be taught the game, but he seemed to settle into it okay. Carla felt a slight chill when it was discovered that Auntie Em's character was the killer, with a rope, in the kitchen for the first round. They all laughed, but there was an exchanged look between Sam and Mary Maude that made Carla confused and a little afraid. Lester didn't seem to notice, but then he didn't display his emotions very much, so it was hard to tell.

Mary Maude and Sam went into the kitchen to make popcorn, leaving Carla and Lester alone. "That was fun," she said.

"That's a dumb game for them to play," he muttered.

So, he did notice. "Really? It's a common enough game. My parents have it, too. I'll bet every household in the whole United States plays this game." Carla was setting it up for another round.

Lester looked at her for a long time before talking softly. She could barely hear him. "This here isn't just any old house. They know what they're doing, and this is a dumb game for them to play with a couple of outsiders."

"I'm family and you're practically like family, Lester. We aren't strangers or anything. They obviously trust us."

By then, Sam and Mary Maude came back into the room with lemonade and popcorn. The rest of the evening was spent happily playing the game, but Carla felt a difference. She glanced at Lester who mostly kept to himself, playing his game pieces, but not making many guesses. Oddly, out of the five games played, only one ended with Carla as the killer. All the rest were Mary Maude. Sam and Lester were never the one.

"Well, you and me got to be the killers all night long," Mary Maude announced as they were putting the game away. "The men just sat by while we did all the work and the winning. The same as life, eh?"

Carla didn't know what to say. It was a game and she was pretty sure her aunt was talking about the game, but knowing what she thought, Carla was unsure if her aunt was boasting about things done or the game. *Wow, you've really gone crazy here,* Carla thought. but, then she also thought about Lester's words and the way he watched Mary Maude during the game, those secretive glances and looks of fear, or something. And the way Sam looked at his wife was odd, too. It was a knowing, sad, creepy look.

There's something going on here behind the scenes, that's for sure, Carla thought. A few minutes later she took her shower and went to bed, but sleep wouldn't come. Carla listened to the normal noises of an old house, squeaking and groaning. Once in a while, she heard the pigs out by the barn or the howl of a cat. An owl hooted in the woods, sounding lonely and making Carla shiver. Eventually she fell into a sleep troubled by dreams of faceless girls and old furnaces.

*   *   *   *   *

Meanwhile, Katie Jean Simons was also worried. She kept trying to call her daughter, Carla, but the phone went straight to voicemail every time. "That just isn't like Carla," she complained to her friend, Norma, who she finally had called in desperation.

"She must be having a great time at your sister's house," Norma commented.

"Hmmmm, I can't believe that. You don't know my crazy sister. She's a real nut job."

"Katie Jean!"

"Well, you didn't grow up with her weirdness. There are times when she looks at you that you just know she's gonna do something bad."

"Like what?"

"Like push your wheelchair down a flight of stairs, that's what," Katie Jean slapped the arm of her own wheelchair." If it hadn't been for Daddy, I think she and Mama would have done away with me even when Mary Maude was still a baby.:

You can't be serious! Then, why on earth did you let Carla go out there to that farm?"

"She's twenty. What was I gonna do, lock her up?"

"Okay, but why did she want to go? I mean, if it's that bad and all."

"Well Em isn't always mean. I mean, at the reunion, she talked it up like that old farm was great and all. She practically begged Carla to come out there and help her take care of the old house. She's never been able to keep help. Our mama had the same problem with nannies and housekeepers. Poor Papa always had to get rid of them, so Mama said."

"Get rid of them? How?" There was alarm in Norma's voice.

Katie Jean looked at the phone in her hand like she just realized it was there. "Well, that's just what Mama would say to him, 'Jesse, that was his name; Jesse, get rid of that girl. She isn't working out.' Something like that, I guess." Papa would drive away with them, back to wherever they came from, I guess..." her voice trailed off in uncertainty.

"And he did what?"

"What? Oh, well I don't know for sure. Took them back wherever they came from, I guess. Isn't that what I just said?"

"Where did they come from? You make them sound like zombies or aliens or something."

Katie Jean waved her hand. "No, they were just from the poorer side of town back then, I think. He probably took them to their homes, you know? There was a place on the south side of town, Mama said, across the railroad tracks where poor people lived. Em used to go with him sometimes, I think, but then he built a sugar shack out in the woods and..."

"And what? You're scaring me."

"What? I don't know, it's just a story. I don't know, triggers weird memories. I was only about twelve when Ma.. when I fell down the stairs."

"But, you were already in a wheelchair, right? I mean, what happened to you on the stairs?"

"I don't know. Just memories of things that are kinda messed up, you know. I just got some bruises and cuts and stuff, grabbed the banister and held on while Mama fell on down with the wheelchair, kinda tumbling over and over." She paused in thought. "Right now, Carla is out there in that old house…"

"Weird,"

Katie Jean laughed. "I know, right?"

"Maybe you're just jealous because she's out there and you're not," Norma offered.

"Jealous? Not hardly! But, I am worried because I know that Mary Maude can be very convincing about things, even if they aren't true. It scares me a little to think that Carla is alone with her."

"Then just go out there," Norma said.

Katie Jean frowned. "Maybe. Well, gotta go. I'll talk to you later." She broke off the call. "Whew! That's the closest I've ever come to saying what I really think." Katie Jean said out loud. "Do I really believe what I think? Papa used to be so kind, so caring. Then he quit coming to visit me, quit even calling. When I did see him that once, he was so sad; sad and tired, and so old. What truly did happen out there?"

Katie Jean got out her diaries from the library bookshelf and lined them up on the kitchen table. "How far back?" She muttered. Carla's twenty, so about thirty years ago." Her hand hovered over her diaries, coming to rest on an old, rust-colored book which she began to read from, leafing through the pages slowly. After an hour or so, she closed the book. She rolled her wheelchair over to the desk to get a pad of paper, a highlighter, and a pen, then returned to the table to make a list.

Names   Positions   Date Came   Date Left   Comments

Three hours later, she was astonished at the length of her list. "And it's not even complete," she muttered. "1…2…3…4…5…….14. My God, why couldn't we keep help?" She leafed through her diaries again, noting more comments about hired help or things her family told her at the time. "Mostly Em didn't like anybody who told her 'no' or what to do. She was so spoiled, that one; Mom's favorite for sure." She looked up at the ceiling, stretching her back. "Was I Papa's favorite, then?" She sat up with a frown. "Of course, he ended up living with Em, so who's to know now?"

Katie Jean sat quietly in her living room for a long time. She knew she should be getting dinner around, but she felt so lost and sad. "How would I even go about finding any of those girls? They would be in their fifties, if they're still living out there somewhere." She looked out the big, picture window, but saw nothing. People passed by on the street, some children were riding bicycles on the sidewalk and her neighbors walked their dog, but she didn't see them. "Why am I interested in this now? Of course, because of Carla, but I've never dug into the past before. I just ignored whatever was happening, whatever Papa was doing. I hid from Mary Maude until Papa took me away. Why? Why did he do that? Was I in some kind of danger?" A quiet voice in her head answered, *Of course you were in danger. She tried to kill you, didn't she? Face the facts. She literally pushed you down the stairs.* Katie Jean was still for a moment. *Is it possible? Did she do something to those girls?* She shook her head vehemently. *No, of course not. That's too deplorable to think of. That would mean that Papa..... And Mama? What about Mama? She couldn't be innocent because stuff started happening to hired help before the stairs incident. And I remember Mama having babies, but none of them lived, did they? Weren't there one or two that cried from Mama's bedroom? What happened to them? Oh, I can't think about this any more!* Tears poured down Katie Jean's face at her thoughts. She absently fingered the notebook on her lap. Finally, she wiped away the drying tears with the backs of her hands, then looked down at the list she had made. She remembered the rat poison in the kitchen cupboard. And there were some chemicals that Mama kept there, too. Katie Jean couldn't remember what it was called, but she remembered clearly the skull and crossbones on the label. "They wouldn't have…" she started. Fresh tears and a sob stopped her from speaking further. "Surely, Mama wouldn't have had anything to do with poison or, or….. or killing anyone, would she?"

Katie Jean put the list back on the table and began a simple supper of hamburgers and fries. Her husband would be home soon and would want to eat. The chore helped her to process all the stress of the past few hours.

"That all sounds insane, Jean, Frank said as he wolfed down his supper. "I mean, I remember your dad. He wouldn't have put up with stuff like that." He shook his neatly combed head. "Not at all. What started all this anyway?"

"We've got to get Carla out of there," she said in explanation.

Frank stopped eating long enough to give her a look of disbelief. "Did you hear what I said?"

"Yes, did you listen to what I told you? Did you look at that list?" She pointed toward the paper beside his left elbow on the table.

"Where'd you get this stuff?"

"From my journals."

"From… so you waited 20 years to bring up your story?" Frank sat back in his chair, wiping his mouth on a paper napkin and sighing deeply.

"I…I just pushed everything to the back of my mind, I guess. If I even knew what was going on, I mean."

"And you think your parents had a hand in this, too?"

"I just don't know," she stared at her hands on the table, before whispering, "I just don't know."

"What's Carla say? Is she okay?"

"I can't talk to her anymore. Her phone just goes to voicemail. She said that Em didn't want her to use the phone."

"Say, what?" Frank stared at his wife in disbelief.

"Em doesn't like modern things. I doubt she even owns a TV."

"And we just sent our daughter there, why?"

Katie Jean shook her head slowly. "She wanted to go help her aunt after that reunion last year. Em made the old place sound like a palace or something. I don't know. She wanted to go, and she is an adult."

"But, now you think your sister killed a bunch of people, including trying to kill you. You believe your own father helped her or something, and even your mother…"

"I don't know, Frank!"

"Well, I'm just trying to lay it out so we can find logic, if there is any."

"What do we do, go out there?"

"Is that what you want to do?

"No," she shook her head. "I don't want to, but I think we might need to go and check on Carla."

"Hmmm," he answered. "Do they have a house phone?"

"What?"

"A house phone, does your sister have a house phone?"

"Oh, yes, yes she does."

"Do we have the number?"

"Yes, in the desk."

"Okay then," Frank laid his hand on top of hers. "Let's just call out there and ask to talk to Carla."

Katie Jean smiled. "Too simple, My Genius."

Frank patted her hand. "Go get that number."

*   *   *   *   *

Mary Maude was shocked when the phone rang. She was afraid it was Donna Sue's mother again. She let it ring six times before she finally picked up the receiver. "Hello," she said hoarsely.

"Mary Maude?" Katie Jean asked.

"Yeah, who's this?"

"It's Katie Jean," she answered. "I'm wondering if I can talk to Carla."

"Why?"

"Well, because I'm her mother, you know."

"She's busy," Mary Maude answered.

"She told me you don't like her to use the cell phone, so I thought you might not mind if we talked on your phone." Katie Jean pleaded.

"Hm," Mary Maude spat out. She put down the receiver and called down the hallway toward the kitchen. "Carla!"

"Yes?" Carla spoke softly from behind Mary Maude.

Mary Maude turned quickly, fear etched on her face. "What are you doing there?" She yelled.

"I'm answering you," Carla said quietly. She stood on the balls of her feet, ready to run if she needed to. She wasn't sure what this was about and she knew enough to be cautious.

Mary Maude looked intently at her niece, a kind of dawning knowledge flowing over her. *This girl is more like me than I realized*, she thought, smiling slightly. "Your mom is on the phone," she pointed at the wall phone at the end of the hallway.

"My mom?" Carla was surprised.

Mary Maude pointed at the phone. "Well, it isn't my mom."

"Hello?" Carla said softly when she picked up the receiver..

"Oh, Carla, are you okay then?" Katie Jean asked plaintively.

"Yeah, I'm okay. Is something wrong?"

"No, no not now," Katie Jean answered with a sigh of relief. "I just felt you might need your mom, or something. You weren't answering your cell, so I called the house."

Carla glanced at her aunt and smiled. "Well, I told you that Auntie Em doesn't like the cell phone, so I turned it off."

Mary Maude smiled back at her niece and went past the girl to put on a kettle for some tea. They were going to need it.

When Carla walked into the kitchen, Mary Maude was ready. "Did you set that up?" She asked accusingly.

"What?" Carla demanded back.

"That call. Did you set that up with your phone so I wouldn't know?"

"Well now, that would just be stupid of me, wouldn't it?"

Mary Maude was taken aback at the answer. "Okay, then what's the call about?"

"Mom hadn't heard from me, so she called," Carla shrugged. "Moms do that kind of stuff."

"Do they?"

"Yes, Auntie, they do."

"Don't you lie to me or sass me back!" Mary Maude shook a spoon in the air.

"I have no reason to lie or to sass you. I am simply explaining what happened. You hear what you want to hear." Carla took a sip of the tea her aunt had poured.

"What did you tell her?"

"About what?"

"About me. About what you do here?"

"Auntie," Carla set down her cup and looked directly at Mary Maude. "What is there to tell? I came here to help you with this house, and that's what I do. Mom knows that. She just wanted to hear my voice. Now she has." Carla sat back in her chair, watching her aunt.

Mary Maude sat back in her chair as well, trying to relax. "Do you want to go home?"

"Not if you need me."

"Hmmf," Mary Maude snorted.

"Auntie Em," Carla began. "I know things happened a long time ago." She held up her hand to stop her aunt from replying, shaking her head gently. "I don't know details and I don't need to. But, I know you and Mom didn't get along very well." She paused, but Mary Maude remained silently sipping her tea. "Whatever happened, it had nothing to do with me. Heck, Mom and I don't always get along either. Maybe it's just the way it is."

"Is she mean to you?"

"Mom? No, no nothing like that. I'm probably the problem. I don't always do what I should when she wants it done."

Mary Maude smiled, almost wickedly. "Well, you do just fine here. I think you are a good girl. I'm sorry I sometimes snap at you. Most of the girls who have come here have been tramps or whores or who knows what all. And liars! They were awful liars. They didn't work out. I got tired of them; that is, I got tired of the way they acted, and they had to go. Tiresome, tiresome girls."

"I'll try not to be tiresome," Carla said with a weak smile.

Mary Maude laughed under her breath. "If I ever think you're tiresome, I'll ship you back to your mother. Then we'll see who's the better mother-figure, huh?"

Mary Maude's booming laughter caught Carla off guard. She didn't know if she should laugh along or cry. She thought about the journal hidden in her room. It told a gruesome and different story of her aunt; one Carla didn't want to believe, but it sounded very convincing. That, added with what she was learning just by living here and things her mother had told her or hinted at.

Mary Maude got up and started to turn away from Carla, but stopped and looked pointedly at her. "You know, I've grown very fond of you, Carla."

Carla didn't know how to respond. Her aunt looked fierce, as usual. But, her words were soft and clear. "I love you, too, Auntie Em. That's part of why I'm here." Carla could barely swallow because her throat suddenly felt tight with emotion. *Is that a tear?* She asked herself as she gazed at her aunt. *Is she really that emotional? I've never seen her like this before.*

Mary Maude cleared her throat and turned away from her niece. She used her apron to wipe quickly at her face, wiping away the tears spilling from her eyes. "Things need done, " she said with a slight cough.

Carla smiled as she got up to clear the table. "Of course they do," she murmured.

*   *   *   *   *

A few nights later, when Carla couldn't sleep, she got out the old diary to finally read it. There weren't many pages written on, but Carla was curious to know about this part of her aunt's life.

Ellie's Diary

Feb 23rd

I came to work at this grand old house. Well, it looked grand from the front, but it is really old and run-down out back. The inside needs a lot of paint and fixing, too. The old man tries, but he doesn't do a very good job. The old woman is kinda creepy. I hope she doesn't yell at me and stuff.

First night. We'll see how things go.

Mar 2nd

I don't get any time to myself. The old woman barks out orders and makes me clean stuff that doesn't even need cleaned. I dusted the living room four times in one day! There's a stain on the hardwood floor at the bottom of the stairs. I dream that it's blood and something terrible happened here. But, it's probably just oil or something. The old man isn't too careful about taking off his work boots when he comes in. Not that he comes in the front door ever. He's kind of creepy, too, but in a sad way. He keeps a beautiful flower garden, but I'm not allowed out there. I see him sitting on a bench out there sometimes and I think he's crying into his hands. Maybe he's just snoozing. I better get to bed. I'm sure I'll have to wash all the walls or something like that tomorrow. Don't know if I'll last long here.

May 19th

I found some old papers tucked into the wall in the downstairs closet. I don't know who wrote them, but they're freaking me out! One said: "She's gonna kill me." Another one said: "I know she killed other girls before I got here. The old man mumbles in his sleep." Another: "There's a big furnace out in the woods. And an operating table and knives and stuff. What is really going on here? I have to be careful not to wake anybody when I sneak around at night." Another: "I'm hiding in this closet. I hear her calling my name like we're friends or something. There's no place to go, no one to call for help."

45

That was the last note. I don't know what to do about them, so I stuck them back into the crack. There's a stain on the bottom of the carpet near the closet door. Don't ask how I know. If you are reading this, I might be dead, too.

July 4th

Maybe I was all wrong. I don't know. For my birthday last month, they let me go to the mall by myself. I had a lot of fun. Then, tonight, we watched the fireworks and Mary Maude said she remembered liking them when she was a little girl. She smiled at me, a real smile. I must be paranoid or something. I just don't know what to make of the notes in the closet. Are they just fakes, or what?

July 24th

Surprise! Another girl came to work here, today. She's younger than me, maybe fifteen or something. Her name is Donna Sue. I love having the company, but I'm careful not to have too much fun. I get to teach her what to do and that makes me feel important and like Mary Maude cares about me.

Aug 5th

Mary Maude wants us to go to the local 4-H fair. I can't believe it! Donna Sue and I are going to help Mary Maude make some strawberry jam to enter in the community food contest. I don't know what we'll do there. I don't have no money and I'm sure Donna Sue don't either. She's older than I thought, eighteen, the same as me. She sure looks younger and acts like it, too.

Aug 6th

The fair was so much fun! Mary Maude gave us each $50.00 to spend. It was amazing! We went on rides and won some fair stuff. I got a big, pink dog and Donna Sue got a huge alligator. I slept in this morning, but Mary Maude just laughed when I got to the kitchen. I'm so confused. When I *clean, I check on the papers in the closet. They are still there. What the heck? Did she plant them like some sick joke or something? I can't ask her about them. If they're real, that would be stupid of me, like I could be in real danger. I don't know what to do.*

Sept 10th

So much work! Learning about gardening and canning and drying foods. It's all useful, I guess, but it's hard work. And Donna Sue whines all the time. I try to stop her, but she is quarrelsome and makes a scene. It's making Mary Maude mad at both of us. She took a stick and beat us both with it today, out in the garden because we dumped a bushel of tomatoes on the ground. Donna Sue yelled at her and hit her back really hard. It might have broken Mary Maude's arm, but she didn't stop or cry out or anything.

Sept 11th

Yep, Mary Maude has a broken arm. It's in a sling and has some boards on it to keep her from using it, I guess. She and the old man took care of it themselves. Weird. They never even talked about going to a doctor. My Mom would have had me at ER in a heartbeat! Donna Sue is locked in her room. We can all hear her crying and screaming in there. They won't put up with that for long. Probably, Sam will take her back wherever she came from real soon.

Sept 14th

She's dead. I came down the hallway just as she went over the banister to the floor below. Mary Maude looked at me and said "She tripped." Just like that. I'm pretty sure Mary Maude could have pushed her, but I didn't see it happen. I just nodded and went about my chores. At dinner, when I was cooking, Mary Maude stood next to me with her good hand on my back. She didn't talk and neither did I. We just stood there for a while. Then she went to the dining room to eat supper. The old man took the body away. I don't want to know where. No more Donna Sue. Freaky. Without her crying and complaining, the house is just quiet and spooky.

Sept 16th

There's been smoke coming from the old smokestack out in the woods for two days. I won't ask what it is. I don't want to know. Donna Sue is gone, and I just keep my mouth shut. I will try to escape some night, I think. But, for now, I have to clean out her room. I won't cry in front of Mary Maude. It might make her mad at me.

Oct 31st

Halloween already. I don't know where the time went. Mary Maude gives out apples from the orchard for the children who come to the door. I have to remind myself that the house looks normal from the street. Mary Maude seems to know some of the parents, and they talk about the weather and things that are going on in town. Maybe I'm just crazy and I dreamed that there was a Donna Sue here. Soon it will be Thanksgiving and then Christmas and Mary Maude is already making plans. She has a whole room full of decorations that she wants to put around the house. The old man is going to get a tree to decorate. Again, I'm so confused. I'm scared and happy and weirded out all at once. The papers are still in the closet. I checked. I don't know what to think.

There was no more. Carla checked in other parts of the closet, but could find nothing except the expected pages stuffed in a crack in the wall. They weren't really hidden, but a person might not notice them if they didn't know. Who left those? What happened to Ellie? Carla felt sick to her stomach and wanted to go home. She thought about secretly calling her mother, but she was afraid that her aunt would somehow know. "This can't be true," she whispered to herself. "Maybe this Ellie was playing some kind of game and I've just fallen into the drama." Carla put the papers from the closet into her underwear and walked swiftly to her room to hide them with Ellie's diary.

CHAPTER FOUR

Finally, a day came when Mary Maude announced that she was going to go to town, alone. "You don't want my help?" Carla asked, looking as innocent as she possibly could.

"You have work to do," Mary Maude said flatly.

"Yes," Carla nodded, looking down at the floor.

"I need some stuff," Sam said quietly from the doorway.

Mary Maude turned toward him with a deep frown. "You plan to leave Lester here alone?"

Sam nodded toward Carla. "She can fix him something to eat. He has chores and is fixin' to work on the back of the house today."

"Bout time," Mary Maude mumbled. There was an awkward silence. "Okay, then. Carla, there's some tomatoes that need tending to, so you got lots to keep you busy."

"How long you gonna be gone?"

"As long as it takes." Was the curt reply.

Carla nodded. Her head was already whirling with the freedom of being on her own for a few hours. She wanted to look at the 'sugar shack' and she wanted to snoop around the farm and orchard. This was the perfect opportunity. Finally.

About an hour later, Carla watched the car go slowly down the driveway and turn onto the street. It crawled up the street while Carla felt that it took forever to get out of sight of the house. She went out the back door and looked around. Lester had been working on the old porch and painting the house. It looked much better than the last time Carla had been out back. He'd pruned up some weeds, too. It looked like a real lawn with a garden and orchard reaching out towards the woods to her left. On the right, was the barn, closer to the house.

Carla walked slowly toward the barn and poked around the old building. It looked all right, what she imagined a barn should look like. She could see where horses used to be stabled and it looked like there used to be a shed on the back for some cows or something. There was a tractor and some other equipment, a big old wheelbarrow that was stained and almost worn out.

Outside, she looked for a while at the pigs. They made a lot of noise and acted like she should feed them or something. She reached out and patted one on the back, scratching its hairy body. It scared her when another pig jumped up and acted like it was going to bite her. Carla jumped back from the fence, stifling a scream.

"You shouldn't be out here," Lester had walked up behind her without her knowing.

Carla blurted out, "That pig tried to bite me!"

Lester smiled as he picked up his ballcap, rubbing the back of his balding head. "Yep, these here hogs is mean. They been fed meat, you know. Whenever the old man kills one, the others get the stuff that can't be used…among other stuff." He winked, which confused Carla.

"I thought Sam burned all the extra parts and stuff," she pointed out at the woods.

"Yeah," he said. "Some of it gets burned up, that's for sure. Spreads the ashes out over the garden and flowers, you know?"

Carla shuddered, thinking of all the vegetables she had eaten. What was in the soil? Did it leach into the food? She shifted position so she couldn't see the pigs. There was no getting away from their noise. "Can we go for a walk?"

Lester shrugged. "Don't think they want nobody out there in the woods," he said slowly.

"Have you ever seen the lake?"

"What lake?" He frowned and spit some brown liquid onto the dusty soil. "You mean that little old pond out yonder?" He pointed toward the woods.

"Yeah, can we take a walk to the pond?"

Lester scuffed the soil with the toe of his boot. "I dunno, Carol. I don't think Mister Sam would like it."

"My name is Carla, not Carol, Lester." She shook her head and started to walk toward the woods. "I can't waste any more time," she mumbled to herself. "I don't know how long they'll be gone."

"Well, Miz Carla," Lester stammered. "I ain't gonna risk my job, so if you get into trouble, it ain't my fault." With that, he walked toward the house where he picked up a bucket full of tools. Soon, Carla heard the pound of a hammer. "That could match my heartbeat," she sighed as she trotted along a grassy path. She got to the "sugar shack" and was surprised at how normal it looked. It was a small building in good repair, better than the back of the house, for sure. She looked in the windows, but couldn't see much inside. Carefully, Carla opened the door and looked around. There were two rooms, one with tools and barrels; the other housing a huge old furnace with a conveyor or something to put things into it. There was also a very old surgical table against the far wall next to a deep, double sink. Knives and tools Carla had never seen before hung above the table. There was a bench with a large grinder which made Carla frown. What would they be grinding if they were burning up old carcasses and stuff? There were five or six tall buckets sitting in a row along the front of the table and a large, spouted urn. It looked like it had some ash or dust in it, but everything else was wiped down and swept clean.

"Get yourself out of here!" At first, Carla thought it was Sam, but was relieved to see that Lester had followed her into the building.

She cleared her throat nervously. "This must be the old sugar shack, huh?"

"Get out," he repeated. "Don't never come back out here."

"Why?" She asked, peering closely at him. He appeared older than she thought and there was something about him she couldn't place.

"You ain't got no business out here. Mr. Sam is gonna have my hide if he ever finds out I didn't kick you out!" As he spoke, Lester's voice got louder and higher in pitch. He seemed to be shaking with anger or worry, Carla couldn't decide which.

After staring at one another for what seemed like a very long time, Carla pushed her way past him and fled out the door. She hadn't been scared of Lester until that moment. She mumbled to herself all the way back to the house. "It doesn't look like they make any maple syrup out there. The things Ellie talked about must be true. I don't know what to do." She shivered in the hot afternoon sun. "It's just an old furnace, not a stove to cook down sap into syrup." She stopped and looked back from the relative safety of the garden. "It's a crematorium, I think." She shuddered at the thoughts filling her brain. "Oh, Ellie, what happened to you?" She whispered, looking around her at the beautiful flowers. "Are you right here in this garden?"

Carla looked at all the beautiful blooms, every color you could imagine. Right in the middle of the flower beds were white roses. Carla made her way through the garden maze to the middle. There was a handmade bench she sat on for a moment. Under the white roses was a rather large stone. Carla stood and walked closer, peering under the bushes at the stone, then squatting down to read the inscription. "Ellen McIntyre," she read. There was no date, just the name. Under it was carved "Jesse McIntyre." Carla touched the names with her finger. In the dirt, almost hidden from view on the left of the stone were two thick wooden crosses. Carla frowned at the names. "James Barnes and Harold Barnes. Who are they?"

"That's Miz Maude's and Mister Sam's boys what died," Lester spoke softly from behind her.

Carla shielded her eyes to look up at Lester. "I had cousins?" She sounded shocked to her own ears.

"Looks like," Lester replied.

"These are my grandparents," Carla caressed the stone again.

"Yes, Ma'am."

"Did you know they were buried out here, Lester?"

"I did. Mister Sam showed them to me special. I keep the markers cleaned off for him."

Carla stood up. Her head was reeling with all she'd seen this day. It was so confusing. She remembered Ellie saying she had the feeling of being confused, too.

Carla went to her room to look for her phone so she could call her mother. The phone was gone. She looked through everything, checking for the diary in the top of her closet. It was still there, so she went back to looking for her phone. "This is why she trusted me to stay alone. She took my phone. She came into my room and took my phone." Carla didn't know if she should be mad or scared. She went to the kitchen where she baked a cake, then started on spaghetti for dinner. She needed to think, but also needed to distract her thoughts from getting too carried away. "I don't know what to think about," she said aloud to the browning meat. Tears dropped into the skillet, but Carla didn't notice. She sniffled, trying not to scream or cry out loud. Only about an hour later, she heard the old car come bumping up the driveway. She said a silent prayer that Lester wouldn't talk to Sam about this day.

Mary Maude was surprised when she came into the house and found that supper was done. There was even a cake! "My, you've been busy," she said to Carla in a friendly way.

"Yep," Carla replied, trying hard not to look at her aunt.

"What's wrong?" Maude always went right to the point.

"Nothin', just nothin'," Carla answered, tearing up at the lie.

"Now, you're lying to me, Carla. What happened while we were gone?"

Carla thought for a moment before she confessed. "I, well, first off, I didn't get the tomatoes done 'cause I went out to the barn and one of the pigs tried to bite me," Carla looked at Mary Maude, then down at the floor. "I knew you'd be mad that I went out there, but I didn't know they would be mean..." she trailed off.

"Why?"

"Why?" Carla asked weakly.

"Why'd you go out there?"

"Oh. Well, I just was on my own and was curious. I've never been around pigs. They seemed like pets or something." Her voice petered out at the end. "I didn't know they would be mean," she repeated.

"Stupid girl," Mary Maude said, but she didn't yell. She didn't even sound mad.

When I picked the tomatoes, I walked around the rose bushes, too." Carla confessed. "I found the graves near the white roses." Tears came partly because she was lying and partly because she really did feel bad for her aunt. "I'm sorry, Auntie Em. I'm sorry for looking around. I know you like your privacy. And, and, well, I'm sorry that you lost your little boys. I saw their markers there next to your parents."

Mary Maude stood silently listening to the confession. She too, was lost for words. She'd never even been out there. She'd never seen the markers where Sam put her parents and their sons.

"I want to go home, Auntie Em," Carla said, breaking the silence. "I just want to be with my mom for a while."

Mary Maude was shocked. "So, you get scared and you just leave me in the lurch?"

"No, I don't want to go home permanently. I just need my Mom for a little bit."

Mary Maude didn't answer right away. "I don't understand that, Carla."

"No, I suppose not," Carla mumbled.

Sam walked into the kitchen. "Okay to eat?" He looked from Mary Maude to Carla, and back again. His smile turned into a frown. "Trouble?" He asked, lines creasing his forehead.

Mary Maude waved him away. "No trouble," she said. "Go eat your dinner. We'll be along shortly."

He went back to the dining room and both Mary Maude and Carla heard him tell Lester to "Sit down and eat, then."

Mary Maude never looked away from Carla and Carla didn't look up from staring at the floor.

"How long?" Mary Maude asked.

Carla sighed in relief. "Just a few days, Auntie Em. Just a few days." She glanced up at her aunt.

"Well, I suppose then," Mary Maude sighed before going into the dining room.

Carla didn't know whether to laugh or cry. She felt relieved, but also suspicious that it was too easy. She didn't go to the table to eat but instead, began doing up the dishes from cooking the meal. She heard the door creak open and turned to look at her aunt.

"You coming to eat?" Mary Maude asked.

"No, I'm not hungry, really. I want to call Mom and get a ride home."

"Sam will take you." Mary Maude disappeared behind the door.

Just like that, after dinner, Sam took Carla to her home. She packed only a few things so Mary Maude wouldn't worry that she wasn't coming back. Carla didn't ask for her phone, but Sam handed it to her when they got into the car. "Thanks," she said. Sam nodded.

They didn't talk. Two and a half hours, and he didn't say a word. Carla didn't know what to say to him, so she looked out the window, played the

A-B-C game, counted yellow cars, whatever she could to make the time pass.

"Thank you, Sam," she said when he pulled up in her mother's driveway. Again, he nodded at her.

"She said to pick you up on Monday," he said as Carla opened the door.

"Monday," Carla nodded at him. "Okay, then. That gives me a few days. Okay, do you know what time you'll be back?"

Sam rubbed his stubbly chin. "I reckon about supper-time. She wants to come and eat out at a fancy McDonalds or something."

Carla smiled. "Okay, I'll look for you on Monday." She shut the door firmly as she got out. He backed down the driveway and drove slowly away as she stood still to watch him go.

Dad's car was in the driveway, so Carla knew her parents were home. She walked in the door without knocking. "I'm home!" She called into the quiet house.

"Carla?" Her mother screamed from the bedroom. "Carla, is that really you?"

Carla ran to her mother's side, hugging and being hugged. They cried together and Carla knelt on the floor, just reveling in her mother's love.

CHAPTER FIVE

Mary Maude was angry at Carla for leaving. "Spoiled brat!" She hissed to the laundry she was washing in her basement. She used a wringer washer and the work was tedious. *It's just what I need, this bunch of dirty clothes,* she thought. She jerked the wringer around to run the clothes into clean water in the double sink. She left the clothes to soak in the cool water and went upstairs to have a cup of tea. "What's she telling her mother?" Mary Maude looked out the kitchen window, through the porch and out toward the garden. Sam was mowing the yard. Mary Maude watched him moving slowly along on their old rider. When the kettle whistled, she moved it off the fire and turned off the stove. She prepared two cups, with plenty of sugar. Then she went out into the yard and offered one of the cups to Sam. He stopped the mower to sit with her in the garden chairs at the back of the house.

Sam looked carefully at his wife. With a sigh, he asked, "And so?"

"What you expect she's really doing?"

"Now, Maudie…" He began.

"No!" She snapped. "Something happened, I just know it!" She took a sip of tea. "Did you talk to Lester?"

"Yep," he nodded.

"Well, what'd he tell you?"

"Nuthin," he coughed and spat onto the ground.

"He saw her out here with the pigs?"

"Yep."

"What was she doin', I wonder."

"Mebbe nuthin."

"Do you believe that, Sam?"

"Well, she's never been trouble before, has she?" He didn't let her answer. "And she's family, Maudie. You got to tread carefully with this one, you know?"

Mary Maude looked closely at him. Sam stared back at her before taking another drink from his tea. She finally looked away, toward the flowers, waving gently in the breeze. "Your flowers are beautiful, Sam," she said quietly before taking a drink herself.

Sam nodded. "Yep," he almost whispered.

"I made a death paper for Papa," she said thoughtfully.

"Oh?"

"Yes, I did and it looks perfect, just like Mama's." She smiled as she thought of the work she had done with her computer. "Carla helped me and it wasn't too hard."

"You're not makin' no more, are you?" Sam frowned at his wife. "I mean, well, we always agreed to say them girls run off, you know."

Mary Maude waved away his worries. "Just one for that fella that dropped himself on the fence. I had his ID card and stuff, so I made one for him. That's all."

"Hmpf," Sam shook his head. "Then leave it alone, Maudie, okay?"

"I'm not stupid, Sam!" She snapped at him. Then she added. "Oh, I don't know Sam, I might make one for each of the boys, you know?" with that she walked away.

Sam was quiet. He knew better than to get Mary Maude angry. He took another drink of his tea and poured the rest onto the ground. He looked up and yelled after her. "You are one of the smartest people I know. But, you leave this alone now. You and me both know what we done and it's over with. You got Carla here now, and she's family. Don't you go getting yourself riled up, you know? We got a good thing going, now. Lester, he's the best of them all and Carla is, too." He stood up, stretched his arms high over his head, arching his aching back, and returned to his mowing.

Mary Maude sat on a bench in the sunshine for several minutes, her eyes closed, listening to the soothing sound of the mower. *Maybe he's right,* she thought. She brushed a fly away from her face and opened her eyes. *But, what if Carla was snooping around? I don't know what's out there in that shack. What if she went out there? Would Lester lie about that? Of course he would!* She snorted aloud. *What is out there? I've never been out there, myself. I never wanted to know so I just pretend it doesn't exist.* She rose slowly and walked carefully through the paths in the flowerbeds. Her footsteps slowed even more as she approached the white roses. Tears clouded her eyes before she could look down. She wiped at her face with her apron and kneeled down to see better. *There it is, then. Papa, Mama, and the boys, James and Harold.* She ran a hand over the engraving on each marker. A chill ran down her back and the backs of her arms, raising gooseflesh in its path. Mary Maude looked up toward the trees, stood abruptly, and walked away from the graves. She found the path that wound into the woods and followed it until she could see the old building. It was in better shape than she imagined. She peered in the door and was further surprised that it was so clean.

She hadn't realized that the mower had stopped until Sam came up behind her and asked, "What you doin' out here?"

Mary Maude spun around with her hand up in a protective gesture. "Oh, Sam," she breathed. "You scared me."

Sam laughed gently, reaching up to push back a stray lock of her hair. "You never been out here before, Maudie."

"I know," she nodded. "It's a fine shed, Sam. I thought it would be dirty and stuffed with junk." She smiled at him, a rare occurrence. "The graves are fine, too." Her husky voice had become a whisper.

Sam rubbed her back with his right hand as he opened the door to the furnace room. "Even better in here," he said.

Mary Maude looked around. The walls and floor were white-washed and everything looked fairly clean. She ran a hand absently along the coffin slide that ran into the furnace. "So this is where Papa began this grisly business," she commented.

Sam nodded. He pulled Mary Maude to him and kissed her neck. "I kinda like havin' you out here, Maudie," he breathed.

"Now, Sam," she hugged him close.

Sam walked her to the operating table and lowered it. He sat down and motioned for her to join him. She hesitated, so he reached out and pulled her by the hand, to him.

Mary Maude laughed aloud. It was a strange sound from inside the old building.

Lester closed the outside door and walked away, laughing to himself. "They are the craziest people I ever met," he said as he walked away, shaking his head. "Crazy!"

*　*　*　*　*

On Sunday morning, the doorbell rang. Mary Maude frowned at Sam. "What in the world?" She questioned. "Carla wouldn't ring the bell."

Sam got up from the breakfast table to peer out the window next to the door. "It's the police, Maude," he said before he answered the door.

Mary Maude stood behind Sam with the screen door between them and the three people who were standing on their front stoop.

"Samuel Barnes?" The policeman asked.

Sam nodded.

"Are you Mrs. Barnes?" He looked past Sam at Mary Maude.

"What do you want here?" Mary Maude asked abruptly.

The policeman pointed at the people with him. This is Ms. Parker from the Department of Children's Protective Services, and Jane Whitman," he introduced the two people with him.

"Okay," Mary Maude said. "What's this about?"

"Donna Sue!" Jane Whitman said loudly. "You know who I am! Where is my daughter? What did you do to her?"

Mary Maude scoffed. "That girl done run off, I already told you."

Ms. Parker was trying to calm Jane Whitman. "Wait, Jane," she was whispering. "There's a right way to do this."

"Who are you?" Mary Maude asked, pointing at Ms. Parker.

"I'm with child services," she smiled at Mary Maude and Sam.

"Child…" began Maude. "What on earth for? We don't have no kids here."

"Donna Sue is only seventeen," the woman purred like a sick cat as far as Mary Maude could tell.

"Okay," Mary Maude answered.

"Is Donna Sue here at your home?"

"No, like I said, she run off months ago." Mary Maude was getting angry.

"May we come in?" Asked the policeman.

"What for?" Sam asked. He laid a hand on his wife's arm to remind her to stay calm. It would do no good for her to go off like a rocket in front of these people.

"We want to look for my daughter, that's what!" Jane Whitman was close to yelling.

"She ain't here," Sam said quietly. "We already told you this several times."

"Well, we…." Jane Whitman started, but was stopped by Ms. Parker.

"We have a warrant here," Ms. Parker said. "To look through this house for the girl."

"Well, what the world?" Mary Maude looked at the paper the policeman handed her. "You mean you can just come in and snoop around my home? Just like that?"

"Yes, Ma'am," the policeman nodded at her with a slight smile. "We won't disturb anything. We're just looking for the girl. She's missing and we hope to find her."

"Don't you think we would just tell her to come here if she was in the house?" Mary Maude asked.

"That would seem reasonable," the officer agreed.

"We get to look in your barn, too!" Announced Jane Whitman. "You can read that right there in those papers. And I want all my daughter's stuff!"

"We don't have any of her belongings," Sam said as he unlocked the screen door. "She took her stuff with her when she left." Mary Maude stood in the way as the trio tried to come into the foyer. "Maudie," Sam pulled on her to move her out of the way. "They're just doing a job. It's all right, now."

Mary Maude's face was a thunder cloud, her face and neck red and her eyes puffy. She was so angry she wanted to scream. She suddenly wished Carla was here, but maybe it was better this way. She backed herself up to the stairs while they walked around her home. "I'm glad it's clean," she mumbled. "Mama would be so ashamed of me if it was dusty."

"Is this Donna Sue's computer?" Jane Whitman asked from the library. "I think that's her computer."

Mary Maude went into action. She almost ran to the library. "No, that is not her computer," she spat out. "That is mine. She didn't even have a computer when she was here. " Mary Maude began looking through some papers on her desk. She let out a huge breath when she found the receipt. "Here!" She waved the slip of paper at the group. "I just bought this and that copy machine over there!" Mary Maude waved a hand at the printer on the top of her rolltop desk.

The police officer looked at the receipt and nodded. "Thank you, Ma'am," he said. "She bought this about a month ago. Move on." He smiled at Mary Maude, but she couldn't bring herself to smile back. She just wanted them gone.

Sam smiled as he moved up to her and rubbed her back. "Quiet, now," he whispered. "Let's sit at the table until they're done."

"Mr. Barnes, I'd like to have a look in the barn, and then we'll be out of your way," said the policeman as they walked into the dining room.

Sam nodded and stood up again to walk them to the barn. He saw Lester hoeing in the garden. Sam opened the barn door and waved them inside. "The pigs is mean," he said. "So just be careful around their fence." The pigs were grunting and squealing, pacing up and down the fence near the barn. *Well, I wish they would calm down,* he thought.

"I'll give them some extra corn," Lester said at Sam's shoulder.

Sam nodded.

"Excuse me," Jane Whitman called out to Lester. "Who are you?"

"We don't have to know that," Ms. Parker said.

"That's just Lester, my hired man," Sam explained to the policeman.

"How long has he been working for you?"

"Oh, about a few years," Sam said thoughtfully, rubbing his whiskery chin.

"Did you know my daughter?" Jane Whitman called out. "Do you know what happened to her?"

Lester went about his chore of feeding the pigs. He didn't look up or react to the questions.

"Her name is Donna Sue," Jane Whitman continued despite being reminded to stay calm and quiet. "Where is she?"

Lester finished his chore and brought the empty metal bucket back to the barn. He put it into a bin full of grain. Turning to look at them all, he nodded to Sam and said, "I don't know much about the house folks. I work out here and keep mostly to myself. Sorry, Lady." He turned around and went back to the garden.

Jane Whitman came up to Sam and pushed her finger into his chest. "I know she was working here. She didn't like it, either. She wrote me letters and told me how mean you and your woman treated her." She took a breath and started again. "She would have come home, not run off, like you say.

She was a good girl. She just wanted a job and to get herself a car." Now, she had her hand laying on Sam's chest. "What happened to her?" She was crying openly, slightly pushing against him.

Sam felt sorry for the woman. *It's a good thing she didn't treat Maudie like this,* he thought. "I'm sorry, Ma'am. I just don't know. She ain't here. She was here, I know who you mean. She worked for us for a little while, but now she's gone." He shook his head, his hands held out with his palms up.

"Where's her radio and stuff," she asked, wiping at the tears streaming down her cheeks. "And, she did have a computer, too. Where's that, I'd like to know."

"I don't know nothing about any stuff she brought here. She must have took it with her."

"Thank you," the police officer said. "We'll be going now," he laid a hand on Jane Whitman's arm and led them all toward the front of the house and their car.

Sam stood still, just inside the barn door. He sighed loudly as he watched them get into the car and leave.

"She was that little blond thing, wasn't she?" Lester asked. "The one that cried and screamed all the time, 'bout everything." He had walked back to the barn when the group left. Sam looked at him but didn't answer. "No tellin' what a little girl like that might do." Lester rubbed his hand over his head and replaced his cap. "Might be a hooker or anything by now." He laughed softly as he walked to the back of the house. Sam watched him go.

Later, Sam watched silently as Mary Maude and Lester talked at the back door. Mary Maude nodded and looked up at Sam. They stared at one another across the expanse of the lawn for a few seconds before Mary Maude went back into the house. Lester was sitting on a lawn chair, watching them both.

* * * * *

"There's something wrong at that house," Jane Whitman complained from the backseat as they drove away. "My daughter didn't run away. They're hiding her somewhere." She also mumbled softly, "That's probably her computer, too."

"We didn't find anything to support that," Ms. Parker said, turning in her seat to look at the other woman. "She had a receipt, afterall."

"They might be a little odd," said the policeman. "But, I didn't see anything to make me think they're hiding your daughter there." He paused. "And she did have a receipt for that computer. The serial number was right there on that receipt."

"You barely talked to them." She paused. "It's an old house, there could be hidden rooms or something."

"With all due respect, Ma'am, we're not living in a TV movie here."

"Don't you patronize me!" She shouted. "My daughter is missing! I know in my gut that those people did something to her!" Tears poured down her face and she didn't wipe them away. They dripped from her chin onto her pink blouse.

"Jane," Ms. Parker said, reaching back and patting her arm. "I know you've gone through a lot of grief and trauma. But, I have to agree that we just didn't find anything to support your claim that the girl is in that house," she paused. "Or the barn." She sighed. "They admitted that she worked there for a time. I doubt they could pay her very much. Perhaps she really did just run off."

"You read her letters. You listened to that awful phone message she left me. How can you now turn a deaf ear to the evidence before you?"

"I did take note of all that, Jane. I believed you then and I believe you now. But, we have looked at these people and neither of us," she pointed at the policeman and herself, "can see more than a girl who has gone away."

"Don't touch me!" Jane Whitman slapped at Ms. Parker's hand. "Just take me home and I'll do my own investigation. I can't believe you want to take their word for it! Didn't you see how that old woman acted? She was as guilty as hell!"

"Don't you break the law, now," the policeman said to Jane Whitman in the rearview mirror. "I've looked at them. They don't have criminal records, not even a parking ticket. They live there quietly in an old house that she inherited from her grandparents. Let the law handle it."

"Yeah," she sneered. "The law has done so much for me, hasn't it?"

"Jane, please do what's right." Ms. Parker pleaded.

"Oh, shut up," she snarled. "Let me out at the corner and I'll walk home," she pointed at a four-way stop. "I need to have some fresh air."

They did as she said and stopped at the next light. Jane Whitman practically jumped out of the car and hurried down the street toward her home.

"Do you think she's all right?" Ms. Parker asked.

"I don't know. I just hope she won't do something that I'll have to arrest her for." He paused.

"Do you think anything is wrong out there at that old place?" She asked.

"No, I don't. They're an odd old pair, but I don't think they are hiding a random girl or have done something to her. I think they are probably right, and she just ran off. She'd been flirting with living on the streets for quite a while before she disappeared."

"That's true. She could have gotten killed down there with that group by the old railroad station. Or, maybe she ran off to California or somewhere."

"That whole family has some issues," he mumbled.

Ms. Parker nodded, falling silent as she thought about the problem with youth in this small town and the surrounding county. *Too many homeless and unsettled, runaway youth,* she thought. "I wish I could help Jane Whitman, but she is, well, I guess she's difficult, for lack of a better word."

"Or crazy," he muttered under his breath.

CHAPTER SIX

Carla woke up on Friday morning in her own room. She heard the sounds of her parents in the house and it was comforting. She stretched, reaching her arms above her headboard where she grabbed the top of her bed and pulled herself up.

The room was bright and sunny, the pale yellow walls absorbing the sun's rays coming in the windows. Carla admired her white, ruffled curtains with yellow roses, and looked around the familiar room. She breathed deep, enjoying being home. "What am I doing out there at that old house, anyway?" She asked herself aloud. She felt guilty immediately. "Auntie Em is so sad," she whispered. "No children, and living in that old house." She got up and walked to her bathroom. "What happened out there?"

Later, after a shower and some coffee, Carla sat in the living room with her parents. "What is this surprise visit?" Katie Jean asked.

"I just needed to be with my Mommy for a few days," Carla smiled.

"Well, that's good, but what happened?" There was a slight frown on Katie Jean's face.

"Nothing, really," Carla hesitated. "I went out by the hogs and one of them tried to bite me, but it didn't." She paused, confused about what she should say now that she was actually here.

"They have hogs?" Frank, her father looked up from his magazine with a curious smile.

Carla laughed. "Yes, they have six hogs, I think."

"Why on earth did you go out there?" Her mother asked.

"I was curious," Carla shrugged. "And I thought they were more like pets than farm animals. I was wrong."

"And you got bit?"

Carla shook her head quickly. "No, no, no, I did not get bit. But, one of them tried to bite me when I was petting another one."

"Oh my gosh, Carla. I would never touch a dirty old pig."

Carla laughed. "They really aren't that dirty, Mom. And I thought Lester and Sam kept them like you would horses or other pets, or something."

"What do they do with them?" Her dad asked.

"I think they butcher them. We eat a lot of pork at the farm."

"My dad had pigs after I left home, I think," Katie Jean commented.

Carla fidgeted with her now empty cup. "Mom," she began. "Did you ever go out to the sugar shack?"

"The what?" Katie Jean asked squinting at her daughter.

"The sugar shack," Carla said slowly. "It's out in the woods. I think they burn up any left over pig parts when they butcher or something."

"A sugar shack is usually where they make syrup, Honey," said her father.

Carla nodded. "I know, but that's not what this is." She wondered if she should go on.

"Well, what is it then?" He asked, more interested than Carla thought he would be.

"I don't know. There's a furnace and a slide-like thing and a surgical table. I think they do the butchering out there and burn up the remains, like I said."

"Hmmm," Dad said. "That sounds like a pretty serious butchering business."

"Yeah," Carla breathed.

"But what?" Katie Jean asked.

"I don't know," Carla sighed. "Sam and Auntie Em are so strange. I think my imagination is running away with me and I got scared for a moment." She drew a long breath. "So, I came here to you."

Katie Jean smiled. "Well, I'm just glad she let you come home."

"I'm not a prisoner out there, Mom."

"No, I suppose not, but as you said, she's odd at the very least. She scares me, Carla. I wish you'd just come home."

"I think I'll go back, Mom. She's just sad, and kind of creepy, but we have a good relationship."

"Well, I don't know how you managed that," Katie Jean snorted.

"Now, Jean," said her husband.

"She pushed me down the stairs and Mama died because of it," Katie Jean said hotly.

"I know, Dear. But, maybe she's changed from that young girl you knew." He turned to his daughter. "Has she ever tried to hurt you, Carla?"

"No," Carla admitted with a shake of her head. She spun her coffee cup in her hands. "No, but she can be scary when she's in one of her moods."

"What kind of man is her husband?" Katie Jean looked interested.

"He's a quiet guy, spends a lot of time outside in the garden and orchard. I don't know, he reminds me of a homeless guy, but I don't know why."

"I think Dad hired him from the streets, you know," Katie Jean was thoughtful. "That's usually where he got his hired hands, and some of the house help, too."

"Yeah, there's a guy named Lester who works there with Sam, too."

"Doing what? I wouldn't think there's that much to do that they need a hired man."

"Well, Dear, you just said your own father had hired men," her husband pointed out.

Katie Jean nodded in concession to his remark. "That's true, of course."

Carla laughed out loud. "I love you guys," she declared. "I miss you, too." She held up a hand before her mother could plead with her to stay home. "But, Sam will pick me up on Monday, so I will be going back. Really, Auntie Em does need help with that big, old house. Although, she has me dust and mop rooms every day and it gets pretty tiring."

"Mama was like that, too," Katie Jean said thoughtfully. "Our house was always squeaky clean. I think Mama worried that germs and dust would make me sick."

"Guess she wouldn't be too happy with our house then?" Her husband teased.

"Oh, you," she waved him away. "Go back to your reading."

Carla and her mother decided to spend some time shopping and visiting with some family friends. It was an exciting yet relaxing day. Carla felt good about the time spent with her mother. However, Katie Jean often said things about her aunt that Carla found disconcerting and made her a little angry. At one point, Carla had to remind her mother that she loves her aunt and had no desire to have to choose between them.

The following day, Carla helped her parents clean their home and do laundry. "I might as well be with Auntie Em," she mumbled to the clothes she was putting into the automatic washer.

"Don't be condescending, Carla," her mother said testily.

"I'm not," Carla responded. "Believe me, laundry is different out there."

"What do you mean?"

"They still use the wringer washer in the basement and hang out the clothes in the backyard."

"Are you kidding me?"

"Uh, no," Carla stifled a laugh. "It's still a thing."

"I had no idea," Katie Jean said. "I mean, I never really thought about it, I guess." She paused. "Did Mama have to do our laundry that way, then?"

"No wonder she hired others to work for her," Carla offered.

"Yes, indeed." Katie Jean said. After a significant pause, she added. "You know, I must have been handled."

"Handled?"

"Yes, I mean, Mama must have kept me closeted up away from everything in the house. I never saw food being made or laundry being done. I mean, I remember that some of the hired help would dust and sweep, stuff like that, but I never thought about how that big old house was run."

"And before you knew it, your Dad whisked you away." Carla added.

"Yes," Katie Jean breathed, a catch in her throat.

Carla took a breath and plunged in to bring up the conversation she was avoiding. "Mom, what happened to the girls who worked at the house?"

"I've told you that Papa used to take them back where he picked them up, you know, to the 'bad' part of town. I think that's where he got them."

"You weren't there when the sugar shack was built?"

"Well, yes I was. I don't remember anyone talking about it much. But I do remember…." Katie Jean paused before looking at her daughter closely. "What are you thinking?"

Carla shook her head. "I don't know, Mom." She waited to gather her thoughts. "I found a scrap of a diary that suggested that maybe some of the girls died and I just wondered about so many hired girls and them coming and going. Oh, I don't know. I'm probably babbling and not making a bit of sense."

Katie Jean smiled at her only child. "No, Honey. I've thought the same things. But, I don't know enough about the sugar shack, so I'm not sure what happened. Are you saying you think they have cremated some of the hired help?"

"Wow!" Carla said. "That sounds brutal, doesn't it?" *I don't know what I've been thinking. This is crazy when you say it out loud. I've got to quit looking for ghosts, I guess.*

"Carla? Are you listening to me?"

"What? Oh, sorry, I was off in la-la-land, I guess. What did you say, Mom?"

"Are there graves or anything like that?"

Carla shook her head slowly. "No-o-o, well, I mean, your parents, you know. They're buried out there in the rose garden. And the two boys are buried there, as well."

Katie Jean frowned. "What boys?"

"I think it must be their children, Sam and Auntie Em's, I mean."

"They have children?" Katie Jean looked a little shocked. "I never thought anything about her having a love life and children. I never knew." She looked back at her daughter. "You mean their children died, then?"

"Yes, I believe they died as infants or maybe were stillborn or something." She sighed. "They never talk about them, but the grave markers say 'James' and 'Harold'."

"Huh," Katie Jean replied. "James was grandpa's name. I think you might be right." She fidgeted with her cup for a moment. "So, she does have a softer side. I mean, if she and her husband have had children and all."

"I don't think she's exactly a monster, Mom," Carla said.

"And yet you do think that they might have, let's say, gotten rid of some hired girls."

"Well, I don't know, that's just it. There have been 'accidents,' I believe. But, if they, or she did, it would mean that your parents might have done that too, wouldn't it?"

Katie Jean nodded and sighed again. "Carla, get me my pad of paper off the desk, would you? I want to show you something."

Carla got up and retrieved the tablet. On it was a list of names and dates. "What's this?" She asked.

"This," Katie Jean waved it in the air before putting it on the table. "This is a list of hired help we had at home, the dates they came and the dates they left, as good as I can remember."

"You kept a list?"

"No, I went through my diaries and compiled a list." She looked down at the writing, running a finger along the list of names. "I remember most of them. Some were nurses for me, others were maids or teachers."

"Boy, you really went through a lot of hired help."

"Yes, we did and I don't know why except that my sister would just get tired of them and they would be sent away. Daddy took them back wherever they came from for many years."

"Tiresome," Carla breathed. "She calls them tiresome when she gets tired of them being there."

"Perhaps," her mother replied. "Mama used that term."

"And did that ever change?"

"Yes," Katie Jean said thoughtfully. "I think it changed with Andrea. She was my favorite and Maude liked her, too. So, she lasted longer than most. I think Daddy liked her more than any of the others. After she left, he started staying away from home more and more. He might have been drinking or something, I don't know. I was a kid, and not just any kid, but an invalid kid. So, I didn't get to know everything that went on."

"Do you think your father had a relationship with this Andrea?"

"Oh, Heavens, no!" She shook her head firmly. "Daddy was true blue to Mama, I'm sure of that."

But, Carla wasn't as sure.

"It was about that time that I began hearing about this 'sugar shack,' as you call it."

"How were things different?"

"Well, Papa didn't make the trips to town like he had before. I mean, when things didn't work out, the girls just went away…" her voice trailed off as she gulped down a sob.

"Do you remember any of the girls dying?"

Katie Jean began to shake her head 'no', but she stopped and thought for a moment. In her mind's eye, she could see her mother explaining to Papa about a girl who had fallen down the stairs, and another one who had 'gotten sick during the night.'

"Carla, I want you to stay home," Katie Jean pleaded.

"Now, Mama, I'm not in any danger." Carla said. "I'm family for one thing. And she let me come home for this visit. I think I can talk her into making this a regular thing every couple of months." Carla patted her mother's hand. "I like it out there in a perverse way. It's like my history or something. Truthfully, she treats me like I'm her own daughter."

"Well, you're not!" Katie Jean said hotly.

"I know, Mama." Carla soothed. She pointed at the paper. "What are you going to do with this list?"

"I'm not sure. I had planned on trying to find some of these girls and asking what they thought of living in that house, but now that you're home, I'm not so interested in that anymore."

"Because you might implicate your father?"

"Well, perhaps, but what on earth did Maude and Mama do? Whatever happened in that house, Papa took me away so I wouldn't end up one of the statistics, I do believe."

"But he built the sugar shack, you know."

"Yes," Katie Jean nodded sagely. "And I don't think I really want to know what he felt he had to do." She paused. "I mean, if Papa did something, well, I just don't want to know that about him." They stared at one another for a moment. "Maybe that old shack will just fall down and be forgotten after all these years."

Carla held her own comment about how the building is kept in working order. And she now determined not to say another word about the diary or the scraps of paper in the closet. *I need to do some more investigating on my own, before I make a decision I might regret,* she thought.

*   *   *   *   *

Monday came too soon for Carla. She debated about going back out to the farm, but in the end, when the old car pulled into the driveway, Carla was ready to go. *I made a promise and I'll keep it,* she decided.

71

Katie Jean and Frank watched their daughter get into the car from the doorway of their home.

"Jean!" Mary Maude called, waving over the top of the car. "Hello! How are you?"

She sounded so friendly, excited to see her sister, almost.

Carla looked in surprise at her aunt, with raised eyebrows. She turned around to see how her mother was reacting.

Katie Jean sat in her wheelchair, staring at the car in shock. She gave a grimace that was probably supposed to be a smile and waved half-heartedly at her sister. "Hello, Maude," she croaked, her voice barely carrying off the porch.

Surprisingly, Mary Maude got completely out of the car and was walking up to the porch. "Is this your husband? I didn't get to meet him at that reunion." She offered her hand to her brother-in-law. "I'm Mary Maude McIntyre," she announced. "You're Frank, I guess?"

"McIntyre?" Katie Jean quizzed.

"Yes," she put a hand up to her mouth. "Well, what a slip that was! Of course, it's Mary Maude Barnes. Has been for years and years." She let out one of her loud, husky laughs, but it sounded hollow to everyone. Mary Maude turned toward the car. "Come on up here, Sam!" She called. "Come and meet my sister and brother-in-law!"

"We met Sam at the party," Katie Jean said quietly.

"Well, fine!" Mary Maude said with a hurt expression. "You can't say I didn't try to be nice to you, Jean. I never did nothing to get this kind of reception. Stay in your fancy house with your stuck-up man. I know my place, back on the farm, in the country, out of your fancy life." She didn't wait for a reply, just charged back to the car and got in, slamming the door.

Carla was already in the car, so Sam just backed out onto the street.

"Do you see, Carla?" Mary Maude asked, turning to look at her niece in the backseat.

"Yes, Auntie Em," Carla replied, trying to remain calm. "I saw what happened."

Mary Maude snorted. "She's always been like that. She made Papa hate me when we were kids. She was always the favorite, always got her way. I was always the one who did everything wrong." She sniffled, but it wasn't from crying, more of a show for Carla's sake.

Carla stared out the window, wishing she was back home to comfort her mother, or at the farm where she could hide in her room. She wished she was anyplace but in this car with these two people at this time.

As the car slowly made its way down the street, Mary Maude was like a little girl, pointing out stores and landmarks like she'd never seen them before. "There!" She called out, pointing ahead of them. "There's McDonalds! Oh, I can already taste my sandwich!"

Carla couldn't help herself, she had to smile. Auntie Em's enthusiasm was contagious. *This is why you're going back out to that farm*, Carla thought. *Because you love your aunt and uncle and want life to be normal for them.* She looked down at her hands clasped in her lap. *It isn't going to be normal, but you want it to be, for them to be kind and funny in a weird way. For none of this other stuff to have happened, for it never to happen again.* She looked out the window at the countryside sliding by. She couldn't eat because she was filled with dread about what the truth would reveal. *What will I do? Oh, God, what will I do?*

The ride was long and tiring. Carla and Mary Maude both slept until they felt the jerk of the car moving its way through the rutted driveway toward the barn.

"I'll make some tea," Mary Maude said as she got out of the car.

"I'm too tired, Maudie," Sam said, walking toward the back of the house ahead of them.

Carla plodded to the back door, as well. "Is there any cake left?"

"I don't know," Mary Maude replied.

Sam turned from the door, with a sheepish look. "Well, now, I might have some tea if there's cake, too."

Carla and Mary Maude laughed as they passed him going into the house.

Lester walked up to them and talked to Sam. "That there cow had a still-born calf," he said. "I thought maybe the cow wouldn't make it either, but she's pulled through. What you want I should do with the little bull?"

Sam smiled. "We'll have us some veal, that's what," he replied.

Lester nodded. "Thought you might say that. He's already hanging and we can butcher in the morning, if that's all right."

"Good man, Lester," Sam gushed. "Thank you for doin' all that work. Sorry I wasn't here to help you."

Lester turned to walk away, but Sam invited him in for cake and tea. Lester declined, saying he was "too tired to eat."

Carla put her clothes away. She had brought a few extra things from home, so she took a few seconds to admire her closet and make a quick plan for decorating. She ran down the stairs to join her aunt, but about halfway down the stairs, she slipped and fell to the bottom, hitting her head on the bottom step.

"Sam! Sam, come quick! Do something, Sam!" Mary Maude screamed into the night.

Sam was in the bathroom, so it took him a moment to respond. "I'm comin', Maudie," he said, hurrying down the hallway. "What is it?" He stopped in his tracks and stared at Carla laying at the bottom of the stairs. "Oh, Lordie, Lordie," he breathed. "This is bad, Maudie; it's real bad."

Mary Maude had dropped down beside Carla and was holding her head in her lap. "Poor Girl, poor Girl," she crooned. "Just like Mama." Tears splashed onto Carla's face.

Carla moaned, moving her arm up toward her head. "Oh-h-h-h," she muttered. "What happened?"

"Oh, Carla," wept Mary Maude. "You fell on those old steps. Don't move too fast."

Carla was trying to sit up. "Lay still, Girl," Sam said in a husky voice, full of the tears he was pushing back. "Just lay back there in Maudie's arms until you feel better."

In a few minutes, Carla was able to sit up, rubbing a hand carefully over her head. She was also beginning to feel some other soreness in her limbs and her back. She looked up the stairs and back at her aunt and uncle. "Wow," she expressed.

"Oh, Carla, I couldn't stand it if anything happened to you," Mary Maude said sincerely.

Carla looked at her in confusion. There were real tears, and Sam was teared up too. *People who kill other people don't act like this, do they?* Carla asked herself. She moved her head carefully. "I think I can stand up," she said. Both Mary Maude and Sam helped her to her feet.

They walked down the hallway, Carla between them. "Sit here," Mary Maude said. "I'll get the tea and cake, and an ice pack."

"I'm sorry I scared you," Carla apologized.

"No, it's not that," Sam said, shaking his head sadly. "Too many people has fell down them old stairs."

"What you sayin', Sam?" Mary Maude came back carrying a tray filled with drinks and food, a bag of ice dangling from her fingers.

"Them stairs are so steep, they're dangerous," he answered.

"I never thought of that," Mary Maude stopped, looking at him. "You're right, of course. Maybe we should just shut off the upstairs and rearrange the rooms down here." She looked thoughtful as she laid the ice pack gently on the back of Carla's head.

"There's enough rooms, you know," Sam said.

"Yes, that's a good idea." Mary Maude nodded. "Just hold that right there, Dear."

"No!" Carla said. "I mean, I just started to decorate my room. I'm fine, just need to slow down." She laughed without humor, looking at two expressionless faces. "I'll be more careful, I promise. Don't rearrange your lives because I was clumsy."

Sam and Mary Maude looked at one another. Finally, Sam cleared his throat. "Well, I suppose," he said, taking a big bite of cake.

"Yes," Mary Maude answered, sipping her tea.

"I love you two, you know," Carla said shyly. She busied herself stirring her tea and taking a taste while holding the ice pack against her head with the other hand.

"I love you too, Dear," Mary Maude said, patting her niece on her hand. "Do you need something for a headache or anything?"

"Yes, that would be great," Carla smiled.

Carla didn't think she would sleep. She had so many things to think about. But, her injuries and the aspirin she took, caused her to sleep quickly and deeply. She had troubled dreams toward morning and woke up late. She wanted to get up and help Auntie Em, but when she tried to move, she was assailed by pain. She hurt all over 'from tip to toe,' as Mom would say. It was already late, yet no one had come up to get her. She moved gingerly, sitting up so she could put her feet on the floor. "So far, so good," she mumbled. She stood slowly and walked to the bathroom down the hallway. It wasn't as bad as she thought, after all. She was sore, but she could move and get around without too much trouble. When she came back to her room, her aunt was standing by the bed with a tray. "Breakfast?" She smiled at Carla.

"Thanks," Carla smiled back. "It smells real good."

Carla sat in the straight back chair and Mary Maude put the tray near her on the dresser. "You okay, I mean really okay?"

"Yes, Auntie Em, I'm good, just sore in a lot of places."

"Well, you take it easy today. I'll get things done." Mary Maude walked to the door. Once there, she paused and turned back. "I....I don't know exactly what to say." With pleading, teary eyes, she fled the room.

"Auntie Em!" Carla called, but there was no answer. She picked at her breakfast, although she did drink the tea and orange juice. "What do I do?" She asked aloud, looking out the window. Thoughts about Ellie's diary crossed her mind. There were the papers from the closet, probably written by someone named Donna Sue or maybe someone else. "What if," she murmured. "What if Ellie planted all of this because she was angry or hurt or just bored?" Carla shook her head. "Why? Why would she do that?" None of it made any sense. Surely these people who were so kind to her couldn't have done what she suspected. "And what about Mom? I can't just ignore her memories like they never happened."

"Who you talking to?" Mary Maude asked from the doorway.

Carla threw a hand up to her chest. "Oh my! You scared me. I thought you went downstairs."

"No, I didn't. Bin standin' here the whole time." Mary Maude cocked her head to one side. "You goin' crazy on me?"

Carla stifled a laugh. "I don't think so," she replied with a shake of the head.

"What's all this nonsense you're talking about, then."

Carla sensed that her aunt was having difficulty keeping her temper in check. Was this the time for the truth, the whole truth? "This house is full of ghosts, Auntie Em," Carla began.

Mary Maude snorted. "What's that you say?"

Carla put up a hand to stop any more comments. "I mean," she paused to choose her words. "Your mother died on those steps and I believe a couple of your maids, or something, right?" She waited for Mary Maude to nod. "Mom told me about how many maids or teachers or nurses, you know, like that, who came and went. But, I've also realized that not all of those people went back home. They died right here."

Mary Maude stared at Carla for a long time before she spoke. "Well, it sounds like your Mama knows more about it than I do, then."

Carla tilted her head much like her aunt did earlier. It gave Mary Maude a shiver as she realized once again that Carla looked more like her than like her sister. "How's that?" Carla asked.

"You're right about one thing. Mama did fall down those stairs and she died there. That's why it scared me so bad to see you laying on the steps." Mary Maude walked past Carla and stood by the window, looking outside. "Mama's buried right out there," she nodded toward the window.

"I know," Carla said softly.

"Papa used to take the girls away," Mary Maude said in a dreamy voice. "I went with him once, but it was boring and I never went again." She sighed. "Papa wasn't a saint, you know. He built the sugar shack." She turned suddenly toward Carla. "Did you go nosing around out there?" Her eyes were blazing as her anger sprouted suddenly.

"Out in the woods?" Carla forced a shudder. "No, I didn't. I wanted to see the lake, but Lester wouldn't go with me, so I couldn't do that. I think he said that it's more like a pond and kinda all grown over. Not worth the time anyway."

Mary Maude nodded as she took a big breath and began to gain control of her anger, yet her hands were still clinched at her side. "Well, did your Mama tell you about her part in what Papa was doing?"

"What?" Carla frowned. "What do you mean?"

"I thought not," Mary Maude nodded. She smiled at Carla. "She wouldn't want you to know that she and Papa got rid of some of those girls. I don't know if she started him in the cremations or not, but that's what began happening whenever somebody didn't work out, you know? I always thought Katie Jean talked him into building that so he didn't have to go to town so much."

Carla couldn't believe her ears. Mary Maude was blaming Mom for what happened here. Carla didn't know what to say. She was pretty sure that Mom was gone from here before she began to walk with her braces sometimes. How could Mom have had anything to do with it?

"Speechless, huh?" Mary Maude smiled again. "Your Mama could have stayed right here. So, why did Papa take her away so fast? There's more here than you know, Child. It's best to leave it alone and pretend none of it ever happened, right?"

Carla nodded. "Maybe you're right. It sounds like a jumbled up mess."

"Are we okay, then?"

Carla shrugged. "We were always okay, Auntie Em. I just won't let my curiosity and imagination get the best of me."

Mary Maude laughed her deep, booming laugh. "Get some rest, Girl. I'll go do up these dishes." She looked at the tray. "You didn't eat much."

"Yeah, but the drinks were super good. That's all I need for now."

"Well, you get some good rest today. Maybe you'll feel like your old self more tomorrow." She swept out of the room.

Carla sighed as she got up from her chair. She was afraid to speak, even in a whisper. *Unbelievable!* She thought. *Whatever happened, I know Mama didn't do it. Maybe Grandpa did, I don't know, but I believe Auntie Em and Sam are up to their ears in guilt. And I'm pretty sure Grandma taught them all they know, well, at least Auntie Em. I'm not sure about Lester 'cause he's as new here as I am. She practically admitted to me that Grandpa cremated people out there in the sugar shack. I wonder if she realizes that she told me so much?* Carla's head really was hurting. She took some more aspirin and laid down to sleep.

CHAPTER SEVEN

"Well, she knows." Mary Maude told Sam. They were standing outside in the garden.

Sam leaned heavily on his hoe. "That weren't smart, was it Maudie?"

"Oh, I didn't tell her, Sam. Her mother filled her head with some kind of stories and she practically asked me about it right out."

Sam looked at Mary Maude for a long time. Finally, he spit into the dirt and sighed. "Now, what?"

"I'm not sure, exactly."

"She gonna stay?"

"Seems like it. She's up there sleeping now."

"Was she upset-like?"

"Not at all. It was like she just wanted to talk it out and leave it be."

"Huh." He answered. "More like you than you know, maybe."

"I've been wondering," she scuffed at a clump of dirt with the toe of her shoe. "Maybe we can put this old house to work for us."

Sam scratched the back of his head, readjusting his ball cap. "How's that?"

"Maybe we could have us a bed and breakfast here."

"Are you crazy, Woman? You want to invite a bunch of strangers here?"

"Well, it wouldn't be many, you know. We've only got maybe four extra bedrooms, including the room Papa used downstairs."

"And what?"

"Well, it would make us some extra money. Maybe we could live normal now. We've got Lester and Carla and it seems all different someway."

"I don't know, Maudie. I just don't know. You get kinda, well, tired of people, you know? What then?"

Mary Maude laughed softly. "They won't be staying more than a night or two, Sam. What you thinking I am, Lizzie Borden?"

"Who?"

"Never mind," she waved a hand at him.

"Is this something Carla wants to do? Did you and her cook this up?"

"I ain't asked her yet, but I'll bet she'll be all for it. She's a go-getter, that one. Reminds me of myself, she does. You're right about that."

"You're gonna do whatever you want, I s'pose," he went back to hoeing in the beans.

Two days later, at supper, Mary Maude brought up the idea again. "What 'cha think, Carla?"

"Wow, that's a great idea," Carla replied between bites of pork pie. "You'll have to do some remodeling, though."

"What 'cha mean?"

"Well, I don't know for sure, but I think you have to have a bathroom for each of the bedrooms."

"Really?"

"I think so."

"Well, there's three upstairs and one downstairs already. Why wouldn't that be enough?"

"I don't think you can make people share bathrooms, but maybe..."

"There's that old closet between those two smaller rooms, Sam. Can we fix that up for another bathroom?"

"Dunno," Sam kept eating.

"What do you think, Lester?" Mary Maude persisted.

Lester looked up from his food in surprise. "Well, I don't rightly know, Ma'am." His fork was suspended in his left hand as he stared first at Mary Maude then at Sam. "I never been up there."

"Okay, after supper, let's go up and take a look. Between you and Sam, I bet we can figure out something good."

Lester was still staring. He carefully put down his fork and wiped his mouth on his sleeve. He looked at Sam again, who continued to eat like the conversation wasn't going on. "If you want, Ma'am."

"I do want," Mary Maude answered.

So the past is just gonna be the past, Carla thought. *Auntie Em is moving on, it seems, so I guess the sugar shack is just that. If nothing else here, then my coming has stopped whatever was pushing her to do whatever it was she was doing. Huh, a bed and breakfast. That could be exciting.*

"Are you going to get some hired help, then? Carla asked. "Or am I just going to be the maid and all?"

"I'll just pay you," Mary Maude said with a broad smile. "You and Lester can be our hired help for it all."

"Okay," Carla said slowly. "What about taxes and all that? Who's going to do the bookkeeping?"

"What do you mean? What taxes? Taxes for what?"

"Well, you have to be licensed, Auntie Em. People will pay taxes and you will send that into the state, I think. It's a business, so you might have to have an inspector look at the rooms before you can rent them out, a license, and all."

"Good God, Maudie!" Sam said loudly. "We don't know anything about all that stuff."

She sighed. "You're right about that, Sam," she said quietly. "We don't."

"Well, I can probably help with the bookkeeping, I guess," Carla said. "But, I'm not sure if I can do it all." She waited for a moment, but no one said anything. "I mean, maybe we could hire one girl as day labor to help with the cleaning and I can help you, Auntie, with running the business."

Mary Maude and Sam shared a look. "Well, what am I gonna do, then?" Mary Maude asked thoughtfully. She didn't realize she had said it out loud until Carla answered.

"Cook breakfast, of course. Serve it in the dining room, and then there's the dishes."

"We'll make Sam and Lester do the dishes after they get the mowing and outside chores all done." Mary Maude laughed heartily as Sam spluttered and Lester looked like he was scared to death.

Carla couldn't help but laugh, too. It felt good to see them in this setting. She knew Sam and Lester were uncomfortable, but they were smiling, too, into their concentrated eating.

"Mebbe I'll put you to work out in the barn in the afternoons, too, Maudie," Sam muttered. He tried to hide his smile. "You can help Lester feed the pigs."

Lester just kept cleaning up his plate. Later, in the barn, Lester would ask Sam if "that woman was gonna be out here in the way?" Sam would laugh and, with a swat to the back of his head, tell Lester to "relax, it was just jokin'."

Meanwhile, Mary Maude and Carla looked seriously at all the rooms in the house. Carla made a map of sorts, a plan to show where each room would be and what it would be used for. They would have to put in one more bathroom upstairs, which could be shared by two bedrooms. That would mean four rooms to rent out. Carla would move to the small room off the dining room downstairs. Mary Maude and Sam would share the living room, modifying it into two bedrooms. The sitting room would become the new living room with the small library off of it. Lester would sleep in the old pantry/porch room where Mary Maude's father, Jesse, used to sleep. There was a small bathroom he could use. Carla suggested that another bathroom could be added by expanding the closet under the stairs into her room. That way, Mary Maude and Sam could use the main bathroom as their own.

"How much you think it will cost to have the house painted, like by a professional?" Mary Maude asked.

"I wouldn't know, but we could look it up online." Carla answered.

"You aim for us to get that on line thing here, don't you?"

"It would let people know about your bed and breakfast, Auntie Em."

"No TV!" Mary Maude frowned. "I don't want all that new-fangled stuff."

"That's fine, the internet would just be hooked up to the computer and we could use my cell phone as a contact."

"So, this is about you using your phone!"

Carla laid a hand on her aunt's arm. "Auntie Em, this was your idea, not mine. It will make you more successful to advertise online and use a cell phone so it can be answered anywhere, anytime, night or day."

"We have a house phone. They can just call that. It always worked in the past." She moved away from Carla. "No," she shook her head. "No, this isn't a good idea. This is madness. Sam's right. We can't have a bunch of strangers here." She walked down the hallway and into the kitchen, the door muffling her words. "No, no, no, no, no........."

Carla sighed as she looked around the living room once more. "It is a lovely idea, Auntie Em," she whispered.

Mary Maude's first impulse was to make tea. She stood in front of the stove for a few moments, but didn't stoke up the fire box. Instead, she turned around and walked out the back door. There on the single step, Mary Maude surveyed the scene before her. The lawn was mowed and the flower bed looked pretty, although fall was causing the blooms to be fewer. The leaves in the woods were beginning to turn golden and red. "They'll fall soon," she muttered. "They'll fall and die." Shaking her head slightly, Mary Maude walked into the garden where almost everything had been picked and taken care of. There were a few hearty tomatoes and cabbages. "Wonder if Sam picked the carrots yet?" She mused. Idly, she walked along the abandoned rows, looking for the carrots. "There you are," she said. "Nope, he hasn't gotten you all yet. "Oh, and there's a few onions in there, too." She smiled at the find. Once past the garden, Mary Maude walked to the center of the flowerbed. She knelt on the ground and brushed off the debris from her parent's stone marker. "What do I do, Mama?" She pleaded. "Papa isn't here to clean up the mistakes anymore." A sigh escaped her along with a single tear. "Me and Sam are gettin' old, too. Especially Sam." She looked up at the sky, then back down. "Funny, I never thought about that happening." Mary Maude's gaze went to the wooden markers next to her mother's headstone.

Sam appeared at Mary Maude's side. With his calloused hand, he brushed away the leaves from the crosses he had made. "We're gitten old, Maudie," he said gently.

"I was just sayin' that to Mama," she whispered back. "Do you believe in Heaven, Sam?"

He nodded. "I reckon I do."

"Do you believe in Hell?" She whispered hoarsely.

"Probably," he said, nodding again.

Mary Maude looked up at the old house. "I believe that this is Hell," she said softly. "I believe it's all there is."

"You really gonna make this here place into a business?" He asked as she stood up. Sam also pulled himself up to stand beside her.

"No, Sam. Carla wants to put too much modern stuff into it. I just wanted something simple, you know?" she walked away.

Sam watched her go, her shoulders slumped and hands hanging down. It was the lowest he had ever seen her. "She needs something," he thought aloud.

At breakfast the next morning, Sam announced that he had some errands to do in town. "We need anything?"

Carla produced a list, but Mary Maude said nothing. She went about cleaning up the table, ignoring everybody else.

"I'll bring her home a surprise," he whispered to Carla. "I know what she needs."

Carla nodded and watched Sam go out to the car. As he pulled out, Carla began dusting the house, again. She avoided the kitchen where she could hear her aunt roughly cleaning up the dishes. "I wonder," Carla murmured. "I wonder what kind of surprise this will be?" She refused to dwell on the thought that Sam was going to bring a maid into the house and what that would mean. *I can't have those evil thoughts about Auntie Em,* She chided herself. *She's not like that anymore, if anything ever did really happen.* After a pause she continued her thoughts. *Really? Nothing ever happened? There's too much evidence and Mama's memories and all. You know they killed the hired help out here. You know it.*

Hours later, Sam returned with not one, but two hired helpers. One was a young man, about thirty and the other was a girl, about nineteen or twenty.

"What's this?" Mary Maude asked, watching the trio come up to the door. She couldn't keep the hint of a smile from playing across her face.

Carla shuddered. The look on Auntie Em's face was one of anticipation, even excitement. Carla couldn't stand it. This was the look of a hunter watching prey, she was sure of it. "What do I do?" She wondered. The thought suddenly struck her that she, herself, could be the prey. She had been here a long time. "I think I am going to need to visit Mama soon," she breathed.

Kaylee and Jason were going to work outside, Sam explained to Mary Maude. They could bunk with Lester, or maybe the empty room upstairs could be used for Kaylee.

"Outside?" Mary Maude questioned.

"Yep, they're gonna paint this old place up right purty." Sam said with pride.

"That takes paint and tools, Sam," Mary Maude said practically.

"Got that, too. It's all gonna be delivered tomorrow." He pointed at the two people between them. "Then, I went lookin' for helpers. These here folks are homeless and could use a good meal and some cash money."

Mary Maude looked closely at the two of them. "Where's your families?" She asked.

"Don't have none," the man, Jason replied with a shrug.

"Nobody wants me," Kaylee said shyly. "I been on the streets in lots of towns before this one, ever since I was sixteen."

"How old are you?"

"Twenty-two," she lied.

"First mistake, Missy," Mary Maude snarled. "Don't you be lying to me. I don't take well to liars."

Kaylee looked down at the ground where she was scuffing the sidewalk with her toe. "Okay, then, I'm eighteen. But, I really have been on my own for the past couple of years. My Ma died and my step-dad, well he just wanted to use me up, you know? I can do that for myself for money out on the streets."

Jason looked at Kaylee with renewed interest.

"Upstairs!" Mary Maude demanded, reaching out for Kaylee's arm. "Let's get you settled and see how good you can work."

Carla and Kaylee looked silently at one another as Mary Maude led the girl up the stairs and out of sight. "Oh, God, what do I do?" Carla pleaded with her head back, eyeing the ceiling. A cobweb forming in the corner of the room caught her eye. Woodenly, she went to the broom closet and got the dustmop to clean away the web.

* * * * *

A month went by. Jason and Kaylee worked hard on the house. They scraped and brushed and finally painted the entire building. The weather held, cool but no rain or snow. It was perfect for the work. Mary Maude was pleased with how well the pair worked together.

Carla knew another thing about this pair. She heard them in the night, either Jason in Kaylee's room, or Kaylee sneaking downstairs to Jason's room. Carla wondered what Lester did while these two were in the bedroom. Mary Maude seemed not to know about Jason and Kaylee. Or, perhaps she just didn't care as long as the work got done.

When the outside was done, Mary Maude was pleased. Now, the house really looked brand new, again. She bought more paint and supplies and asked Jason and Kaylee to stay on and paint the inside.

Jason shrugged. "Sure, why not?" He looked around the dining room with a critical eye. "Anything else you want done? I mean, the food's good and I could keep busy all winter to have a warm bed and…" He winked at Kaylee.

Kaylee blushed, but nodded her head quickly. "Yeah, sure, I got nowhere else to be."

Mary Maude looked at Jason with interest, seeming to be oblivious to the discomfort of Kaylee or the flirtation from Jason. "Do you know anything about electricity or plumbing? Can you like, remodel this old place over the winter?"

"Well," Jason answered. "It depends on what you want done."

"I'm thinking of adding a couple of bathrooms and reorganizing a couple of other rooms, you know, kind of spruce up the place?"

"Maybe," Jason said.

"Good!" Mary Maude smiled and clapped her hands together. "We'll just start upstairs, then move down here."

Jason shook his head. "You got the money to make all these changes, Lady?"

Mary Maude instantly pinned Jason with a cold stare. "All I need you for is some work, Young Man. Keep your smart mouth shut and we will get along. Otherwise, there's the door, right over there." She waved her hand toward the doorway to her left.

Jason raised his hands and pushed back his chair with a scrape on the floor. "No problem. Just making sure this isn't an empty dream, you know? People say stuff all the time, but don't always come through." He waited, but Mary Maude just continued to stare him down. "I've had some bad experiences with people," he mumbled, his hands on his lap and his head down.

"All I know how to do is paint," Kaylee said in a small voice. "But, I'm good at it." She looked around the table at everyone else.

"Auntie Em," Carla spoke, gently touching her aunt on the arm.

Mary Maude jerked her arm away. "Stop that!" She snarled.

"He didn't mean anything by his comment," Carla persisted. "It's okay for him to have an opinion about other people. It wasn't necessarily about you."

Mary Maude stood up quickly. She pointed a long, bony finger at Jason. "Don't you ever call me Lady again!" With that, she swept out of the room, up the stairs toward her bedroom.

"Thanks," Jason whispered.

Carla smiled. "It's okay, she'll calm down."

"She scares me," Kaylee looked close to tears. "Like a witch."

"Don't ever say that where she can hear it," Carla cautioned.

"Are you coming, Kid?" Mary Maude's voice came from the top of the stairs. "I want to show you what we're gonna do."

Jason suddenly shook his head and laughed. "Yeah!" He called as he got up. "I'm coming."

"Wait!" Carla stood up. "I mean, let me go up first."

"Okay," Jason frowned.

Carla ran past him and up the stairs. Jason and Kaylee followed her.

Mary Maude wasn't at the top of the stairs, but had gone into the extra bedroom. "We'll start in here," she called. When they all trooped into the room, she looked surprised. "Well, what the world?" She said.

Carla stammered. "I, well, I didn't know where you were," she said lamely. "I'm going down to do the dishes then go to bed. I don't feel too good." Carla said weakly.

"Are you okay?" Mary Maude looked at Carla with concern.

"Yeah, yeah, I'm okay. I just need to sort out some thoughts and stuff. Something stupid like dishes will help."

Mary Maude smiled. "Don't forget to mop the floors."

Carla had been mouthing the words along with her aunt.

"Sassy girl," Mary Maude swatted at her, but Carla ran out the door and walked carefully down the stairs. She paused to stare at the stain on the floor at the bottom of the stairs for a moment. *A reminder,* she thought before shaking her head and going to the kitchen.

Once she had all the dishes in the kitchen, Carla ran water to wash them. "You panicked," she said softly. "You thought something awful and panicked." Carla shook her head, her hair bouncing at the movement. "Did you really think she was just going to push him down the stairs or something? How stupid!"

"Uh, Miss Carla?"

Carla swung around in surprise. "Lester, you scared me to death!"

"Yes, Ma'am. I'm sorry." He was twisting his ballcap in his hands.

"What do you need?"

"I was wonderin' if those people are gonna stay for real," Lester cleared his throat.

"It looks like it. I think Mary Maude is going to have them paint and stuff on the inside."

He nodded. "Them two, well, they, uh, they…"

Carla smiled. "I know, Lester," she said softly. "I hear them at night, too. I know what they're doing." She felt a warmth creeping up her neck.

"I'm just sayin' that ole Sam and Miss Maude, they won't like it none when they find out."

"Maybe," she admitted.

Lester shook his head slowly. "Things happen out here, Miss Carla. I mean, well, you don't want to go makin' them upset. It don't go well." He paused. "You and me, we're different. I don't think anyone has stayed here as long as we have. We know how to keep our mouths shut and just do what we're told." He paused again, still wringing his ballcap. "And, course, you being her niece and all, that keeps you safe, too." He looked up at her with a pleading in his eyes.

"I think it's okay this time, Lester." Carla hesitated to say too much. She was unsure herself what all had happened here and she didn't know what Lester might know or if he was guessing. "They are still useful so it's okay."

"Yes, Ma'am, I hope that's true." He turned abruptly and walked out the backdoor. "But, I would like to sleep without the gymnastics across the room," he chuckled lightly as he went out.

Carla let out a huge sigh. "Please let this be okay," she pleaded. She turned back to her dishes. When she was finished, she had a pounding headache. She went upstairs to her room, pausing to tell her aunt "I'm going to bed now."

"Good night," Mary Maude waved at her. She was sending Jason and Kaylee to their rooms, too. "No nighttime shenanigans tonight, you hear me?" She wagged a finger at each of them. "Let us old folks get some sleep for a change, especially Lester."

"What?" Kaylee asked with what she hoped was a look of innocence.

"Yes, Ma'am," Jason smiled with a wink.

Carla just shook her head and went to her room. "So, Auntie knows anyway," she mumbled. A giggle escaped her as she sat on her bed and changed into her nightgown. "We're all worried for nothing. It's over. She's not going to do anything, and I've got to quit thinking along those ugly lines. Who do I think I am, anyway?"

*   *   *   *   *

It took about two months for the house to be finished. Mary Maude just kept buying paint and parts, building supplies, and the like. Jason proved to be talented at building and remodeling. He had some good ideas about making the bathrooms fit for handicapped guests, and he added a second handrail and rubber treads on the stairs for safety. Mary Maude was happy, walking around singing, decorating for the holidays, and cooking up traditional dishes.

For Christmas, Mary Maude bought everyone clothes and gave them each $50.00 to spend as they liked. Carla also gave them all gift cards. Sam and Mary Maude just looked at her like she was crazy when she told them how to use the gift cards. Lester scratched his beard and shook his head at such a thing.

Just after New Year's Mary Maude asked about the internet. "How do you get that online thing, Carla?"

"You contact a provider and sign up. You have to pay for it every month."

"Pay?" Mary Maude asked. "What do you mean? How do you pay a machine?"

Carla smiled. "You can use your bank card or your account to set up payments that will automatically come out of your account."

"So, I write a check, you mean?"

"Well, no…. I mean, you could, but don't you have a bank debit card?"

"No, I don't have a credit card. Them things are no good, just trouble." Mary Maude was shaking her head. "Does your Mama have one?"

Carla smiled again. "Yes, Mama and Daddy both have debit cards. They can use them at the store instead of writing a check or carrying around cash."

Mary Maude shook her head. "And some stranger can just take your money?"

"Well, not exactly. I mean, you give them permission to take your payment."

"No, no, no," she was shaking her head dramatically. "Nobody is gonna get their hands on my money like that. I deal in cash, mostly. But you know I do write some checks for bills. I just want to pay for stuff like that. I don't want no cards or anything."

"Almost everybody uses debit cards, Auntie Em," Carla said.

"Well, I ain't everybody. You should know that by now." She snorted into a laugh.

Carla had to agree. Her aunt was totally different from anyone she ever knew. "Are you going to go ahead with the bed and breakfast then? I mean, you got all the changes in the house. Was that your plan?"

"Nope, I'm not going to do that. Maybe you can someday, but for now, I just wanted the house to be nice and feel like new. And it does! Them two did a right fine job. Even Sam had to agree that it didn't cost so much."

"He thinks the house is too fancy, now though," Carla added.

"I know. I told him to take off his boots and he got all huffy with me."

*　　*　　*　　*　　*

When it came, it was truly an accident. In March, just when the snow was melting off and the temperatures were warming up, Jason was replacing some roofing on the barn. Lester went to get some shingles for him, and while he was gone, Jason tried to come off the barn roof, missed his footing, evidently, and fell to the ground. His head hit a cement pillar sticking out from the foundation of the barn. He was dead when Lester found him.

Lester ran toward the garden where his employer was working. "Mister Sam, Mister Sam! Come quick!"

Sam looked up, shielding his eyes from the sun. "What now?" He muttered.

Lester was waving toward the barn. "It's Jason, come quick! He's hurt real bad!"

Sam walked to Lester and went to where Jason's body laid sprawled on the ground. Blood was running into the grass. "What happened?" He asked calmly.

"He fell from the roof," Lester panted.

"Okay, Lester. Calm down. It's not like nobody never died out here before."

"Yes, Sir," Lester was trying to breathe. "I was just runnin' and I don't s'pose I should have."

"Get the wheelbarrow out of the barn, will ya?"

Lester headed for the barn. Sam grabbed a nearby shovel and scraped up the blood and brain matter to throw over the fence to the pigs. "You all haven't had anything like this for a good long while," he said. "Matter of fact, you are youngsters and probably never had anything like this. Your pappy did, though. He had him a-plenty."

Lester came back with the wheelbarrow and Sam helped him get the body into it. "Take him on down to the sugar shack and start the furnace," Sam instructed. He looked up at the house, but couldn't see Mary Maude in the bedroom window. He headed for the house to talk to her.

"An accident, for real?" Mary Maude asked.

"Yep," Sam nodded.

"Huh, that hasn't happened for a long time."

"I know. But, he didn't have nobody, so I guess we'll just put him in the flower garden. I got Lester heating up the furnace. I'll take the old truck to town for some propane and you can tell whatever story you want about that." He pointed in the general direction of the sugar shack.

Mary Maude nodded. "I'll tell the girl. She won't take it easy. They was having sex together and all."

"Here in the house?" Sam looked shocked. "You were okay with that then?"

"Well, Sam we was young once. And they worked out good, you know? Didn't hurt nothing, did it?"

"I guess not, but in your younger days, that wouldn't have happened."

"I reckon you're right." She waved him away with a sly smile. "Go do what you got to do."

Sam pulled her by the arm and planted a kiss on her cheek. "I will. Are you happier, Maudie?"

"I guess I am," she admitted. "I guess I am." She playfully swatted at him, but he was already walking away.

From the house, Carla saw the smoke from the woods. One, long finger of white smoke reaching up beyond the trees. "Now, what does that mean?" She muttered under her breath. She walked downstairs and into the living room where Mary Maude was talking to Kaylee.

"He fell from the barn roof and it looks real bad."

"No!" Kaylee breathed, tears rushing down her face already. "No, it can't be."

"I know it's hard, but that's just the way it is."

Sam poked his head in from the hallway. "I'm off to town then, Maudie. I'm takin' the old truck."

"Yes, that's good, then, Sam." Mary Maude answered. "Drive careful, but hurry along."

Carla stepped up. "Are you saying that Jason fell from the barn roof? Or Lester?"

"No, it was Jason. He seems to have missed the ladder when Lester was getting something out of the barn, I guess. Sam's taking care of it. There's a hospital in town and all."

Kaylee sniffled. "Why didn't you call 9-1-1?"

"Well, you know we're old-fashioned. Ain't it so, Carla?"

"That's true enough," Carla said with a worried look and a tone to match. *I saw the smoke. I know Sam didn't take anybody to a hospital. Why is she lying to Kaylee? What good will that do? Is lying about these things just a habit?* Carla's thoughts were spinning.

"Well, there's work to do so let's get it done, "Mary Maude said. "Best to keep busy."

Kaylee went upstairs to her room. Carla followed Mary Maude into the kitchen. "What's going on? I can see the smoke from the sugar shack, you know."

"Now," Mary Maude patted Carla on the back. "He didn't have family or anything you know. It's for the best."

"You just lied to Kaylee."

"No, I did not!"

"She thinks Sam took him to the hospital."

"Well, that's her interpretation then. I just gave her the facts. When Sam comes home, he'll tell us all that Jason died, which he did."

Carla let out a big sigh. She went up to her room and braced her door shut with a chair. She got out Ellie's diary and read through it again.

Sept 16th

There's been smoke coming from the old smokestack out in the woods for two days. I won't ask what it is. I don't want to know. Donna Sue is gone, and I just keep my mouth shut. I will try to escape some night, I think.

"Did you escape Ellie? Did you?" Carla asked quietly. She curled herself up into a ball on the bed and cried. She wasn't sure what she was crying about. "I don't even know Jason and Kaylee that well," she muttered. "Ellie's been gone for a long time. I don't even know how long. Maybe she really did get out of here." Carla got up and walked to her window. "Maybe I'll go home for a while. I can't do this by myself. I need to talk to Mom."

When she heard the truck rumble into the driveway, Carla stepped out into the hall and looked over the bannister. Kaylee had fled down the stairs so she could be at the door when he came in. "Slow down, Girl," Carla heard Mary Maude say. "He'll be in directly. He's got some supplies to drop off in the barn and what-not-all." They went into the kitchen, so Carla followed, entering the kitchen to find her aunt making tea, as usual. She could hear Mary Maude humming a vague tune quietly.

Finally, the truck came back to the barn. Carla then realized that he had gone down to the sugar shack. She looked questioningly at her aunt.

"Propane," Mary Maude said with a nod.

"There's tea ready," Mary Maude said as Sam came in the back door.

He looked at all three expectant faces. "He's gone, then," he said as he pulled out a chair and sat at the kitchen table.

"Gone?" Kaylee looked like she might faint. "What...you mean..."

"He died," Sam said without looking up.

"What am I going to do?" Kaylee looked first at Mary Maude, then at Carla. "We were making some plans, and..." She, too, sat at the table.

"You can still stay here and work with Carla," Mary Maude said. "We're not kicking you out or nothing."

Kaylee closed her eyes and shook her head slowly. "Yeah, well, I'm pregnant probably. So, now what?"

"Oh, for crying out loud!" Mary Maude spluttered. "Why wasn't you more careful than that?"

Kaylee looked up with tear-filled eyes. "I didn't plan this, you know."

Carla began a light supper, something they could all just snack on. No one was going to be hungry anyway, so no sense cooking up a big meal. Lester didn't come to the house until late, either. At ten o'clock, Carla put the few left overs away and cleaned up. It was done in no time.

Two days later, Carla announced at dinner. "I'm going home for a bit. I need to be with my Mom."

"No, you ain't!" Mary Maude said hotly.

"I'm not a prisoner here, Auntie Em. I need to think for a while and I can't do it under this roof." She reached out and touched her aunt's arm. "I'll be back. I won't abandon you."

Mary Maude sat woodenly, her back straight. "How long?"

"Maybe a week," Carla answered. Silently, she thought, *She asked, she didn't tell me.*

"Tomorrow's Thursday, so Sam will take you and pick you up next Thursday."

"No, I'll drive myself back."

"You're gonna bring your car here?" Mary Maude looked surprised.

"Yes," Carla nodded.

"Huh ... Well..."

"I'll return. I promise you, in a week."

"Call me on that cell phone thing, will ya?"

"Okay, I can do that."

"Everyday."

Carla laughed lightly. "At least 3 times during the week."

After chores were done, Mary Maude went out to the garden to talk to Sam.

"So, she knows then?" He asked in wonder. "She really does know?"

"Yep, and she's coming back, too. It didn't seem to scare her..."

"She could bring the law, Maudie."

"What for? It was an accident, after all and now he's gone. There's nothing for the law to be here for."

"Did you talk to the girl?"

"I tried, but she's moping around like a lost puppy. Sure hope she gets over it fast. Don't know what to do about a baby."

"What you mean?" Sam looked bewildered.

"Stupid girl got herself pregnant, she thinks." Mary Maude was wagging her head.

"Good Lord, what next?"

"Well, it may not make it. She's in such a state, she might lose it or something." Mary Maude said more to herself than to Sam.

"Lester's sick." Sam said nonchalantly.

"What do you mean?"

"I mean, Lester is sick."

"Who's tending the furnace then?"

"He is, but he's coughing like he's gonna die. Got him a cold or something."

"Oh, well, he'll be all right."

"Probably. Says he packed up all of Jason's stuff and we put his backpack in the furnace, too."

"Good. That's done then." Mary Maude started to walk away. "You gonna hire another man, then?"

"Not now, Maudie." He shook his head without looking back at her. "I…not now."

Mary Maude walked to the house, thinking deeply. *Can you get too old? Papa never did.* She stopped. *Well, now, I'm wrong. Sam was here and just took over. Maybe Lester will do that, too.* She continued her walk. *I'll get him some herbs to make sure he's healthy.* She stopped once again as she reached for the door handle, looking back at Sam hard at work. *Will I get too old? Will I have to rely on Carla to take over here?* She shook her head. *No, no she won't do it. She'll make the old place into a bed and breakfast, that's what. She's the best of both me and Katie Jean. She'll bring her own kind of strangers in, and they won't stay, they'll just go home. 'She might hire somebody'* said a niggling voice in her head. *Well, then she'll have to take care of that. But mostly, this sad old house might just be happy someday.*

On Thursday, after Sam and Carla left, Mary Maude went into Lester's room to give him some home remedies. She knocked on the door and heard him tell her to come in, through his coughing. It really did sound bad.

"You're hacking up bad. I brought you something to make you feel better, some soup and some medicine."

Lester shook his head, laying there on his bed. "Naw, I don't want to take nothin' Miz Maude. "What is that stuff anyway?"

"Just herbs to fight off that cold, cough syrup, tea, some chest rub. Put that on the bottom of your feet, too. It helps real good."

Lester kept coughing and turned away from her.

"Well, I'll just leave it here for you. There's some chicken soup, too that feels real good going down a sore throat. We want you to be healthy, Lester. You're a good helper for Sam and me."

As Mary Maude set the tray on his bedside table, she put a hand on his forehead. "You got you a fever. Here, drink this tea right away. It's willow bark, sure to break that heat that's burning you up."

Lester half sat up and looked at the tea in Mary Maude's hand. "Thanks, Miz Maude." He took a sip..

Satisfied, Mary Maude turned to go.

"Miz Maude?" He stopped to cough again. "Don't let Mister Sam feed me to those hogs, you hear?"

Mary Maude smiled. "No, Lester. We'll take good care of you. Sam needs you out there in the gardens and what-not-all."

"Yes, Ma'am." He took another sip of tea and swallowed hard.

*   *   *   *   *

Mary Maude was trying to talk to Kaylee. "You ever going to do anything but cry?"

"I can't believe he's dead, is all."

"Well, it happens. There's work to do and you and me are it for labor."

"Why'd Carla have to go and leave/"

"That's none of your business!" Mary Maude was getting upset with the girl. "You was working out real nice, and now you just want to laze around and do nothing, day and night. I ain't gonna put up with that, Kaylee."

"Are you kicking me out on the streets again, and me pregnant?"

"Maybe, if you keep getting an attitude with me." Mary Maude sighed. "But, right now, I need your help to keep this place clean. So, get up and get moving."

"Why do you keep this big old house? You don't even use half the rooms."

"That's none of your business, neither. I expect you to come downstairs and help me cook and clean up, that's all."

CHAPTER EIGHT

Katie Jean was again surprised that her daughter showed up at home. "I feel so much better knowing you can just pop in like this."

Carla smiled sadly. "I know, Mom, me too."

"Except there's something wrong this time."

"No," Carla shook her head. "Well, yes and no." She shrugged. "I don't know. I just needed to come home and see you and Dad, something normal."

"She does get to you over time, huh?"

Carla forced a laugh. "I guess you could say that." She stretched. "I want a nice long shower and twenty hours of sleep in my own room."

Katie Jean frowned. "You don't share a room out there?" She questioned.

"No, no, I don't share. But, I don't feel like I have privacy, either."

"Why's that?" Katie Jean was frowning, trying to understand.

"Auntie Em just pops up everywhere, it seems like. She never knocks, just walks in and starts talking, or I'll come out of the bathroom and she is standing in my room, looking out the window. It's kind of creepy."

"She stands staring out the window?" Katie Jean asked in a dreamy voice. "Like Mama used to do?"

"Did she?" Carla asked with interest.

Katie Jean nodded, still thinking about the past. "I didn't realize Maude had picked up the same trait."

"Yeah. She does the same thing in her own room, just stands at the window looking out into the back yard." They stared at one another for a moment.

"How's the remodeling going?" Mom asked, changing the subject and the mood.

"Um, it's pretty much done." Carla thought about Jason and Kaylee. *Not yet,* she told herself. *I have all week to talk about this stuff. For now, I just want that shower.* "Okay if I shower and change?"

Katie Jean smiled as she nodded. She wheeled herself to the kitchen to make a meal for her family.

After supper, Frank and Katie Jean shared their plans to take a vacation together. "We want some memories to pass on to you."

Carla smiled as she half-listened to what her parents said. It was pleasant to just listen to their excitement and bask in the love they shared. *Sam and Mary Maude love each other, too. It's just so different, maybe because they don't have kids, just those sad graves in the garden.*

"We're going out for ice cream. You want to come?" Katie Jean looked hopeful.

"I really don't, Mom," Carla apologized. "Sorry, but I just want to curl up with a book and fall asleep in my bed, in my room, all by myself. You two have fun, okay?"

Carla wasn't sure how long she had slept. There was a constant pounding that woke her, but she couldn't place the sound. It finally dawned on her that someone was at the door downstairs. "Why doesn't Mom just answer that?" She mumbled, fumbling for her housecoat and slippers. She realized it was dark and she was only using the nightlight in her room.

It seemed to take her forever to get to the door. When she opened it, there were two policemen on the other side of the screen.

"Yes?" Her heart was pounding. A thought was forming as the man to her right began speaking. She couldn't hear him because someone was screaming. As she fell to the floor, gentle hands grabbed for her. It would be several minutes later, with the sound of sirens in her ears, that she opened her eyes again.

"Carla, are you okay?" Asked Mama's best friend, Norma.

"It isn't true," Carla whispered, fresh tears streaming down her face.

'It is, Honey. I'm so sorry." She faded away as paramedics took her place and before Carla knew what was happening, she was whisked to the hospital. What happened after that was a blur. Carla slept and tried to ignore the nursing hands that gave her aid.

Finally, Carla opened her eyes to a cheerful hospital room, sunshine streaming through the window to her left. "Well, it's about time you woke up," said a familiar voice. It was Mama's friend, Norma. Carla looked to her right and smiled faintly.

"How long have I been here?"

"Just a day."

"What happened?"

"Well, the police came to tell you that your parents had been in a terrible accident, and you just started screeching at the top of your lungs. I was up letting the cat in and heard you clear over at my house, so I came running."

"Thanks," Carla said sadly. "Both of them?"

"Yes, Honey."

Fresh tears threatened. "I can't believe it…."

"I know, it's real sad."

Carla looked around her. "Do you know where my phone is at?"

"No. Would it be at the house?"

"Probably, and my purse."

"Well, I think they'll let you go home, because you're not really sick or anything. It was just such a shock."

"That's for sure." Carla paused. "I really need to call my aunt."

"That crazy lady where you're staying?" Norma asked curiously.

"Why would you call her that?" Carla asked.

"Your Mama told me some stories about her sister. I don't know why you want to stay there when you have such wonderful parents." Norma was wagging her head.

"I don't know what Mam said to you, but Auntie Em has been good to me. She's kind of a sad person and has lost her own children."

"Did she kill them?" Norma asked innocently.

"What? No! Why would you ask me that?"

"Because your Mama thought that your aunt tried to kill her when they were younger, you know."

"I can't believe she told you that old story," Carla said. "Whatever happened when Mom's mother died, there's no proof that Auntie Em had anything to do with it. I am perfectly safe there and I think of it as my second home." Carla realized that at least that part of the story was true.

Hours later, Carla was on her way back to her home, the cute little bungalow where her parents lived. "Not anymore," she reminded herself in a whisper. As they came down the block, Carla couldn't keep the tears from splashing down her face. *Auntie Em, you're all I have now. Please don't be crazy,* she thought. As soon as possible, Carla got her phone and made the call.

"Hello?" Said the gruff, familiar voice.

"It's me, Auntie Em," Carla said.

"It's about time! Been two days already!"

"I know, I'm sorry." Carla could barely breathe. She was trying hard not to cry. "Well, you okay?"

"Not really," Carla said slowly. "Auntie Em, my mom and dad were killed in an accident just after I got here." She couldn't help it. The tears flowed and her voice broke. She felt like screaming all over again.

Leave it to Katie Jean to get all the attention, Mary Maude thought. "Okay, now, Carla. Just cry it out. You'll be okay. Come on home."

"I can't right now, Auntie Em. I have to figure out the funerals and all that stuff. I don't even know if Mom had insurance or anything. It might take me a little longer than we planned, maybe two weeks instead of one." Carla sniffled, wiping her nose on her sleeve.

"Is somebody helping you? Do you need us to come up there?" Mary Maude sounded genuinely concerned.

"No, I mean, yes, I have help. A friend of mom's is helping me. There's no need for you to come, I guess. I don't know what you would do. I don't know what I need to do." She paused. "I'll get it figured out. I'll keep calling you to let you know what's happening, okay?"

"Well, don't stay there too long. Are you sure you don't want me to come over there?"

"No, I've got Mom's friend and some people from her church, like I said. I'll get it done as soon as I can."

"Keep callin' me, Girl."

"Yes. Yes, I'll do that."

"Okay, then, bye."

"No! I mean, Auntie Em?"

"What?"

"I love you and Mister Sam." Carla cried softly.

Mary Maude choked on the words. "I love you too, Girl. I love you, too. It's like you're my own daughter now. Hurry home."

*   *   *   *   *

Carla was surprised by the amount of debt her parents had. She also didn't know that they didn't own their home. "I think I owe the bank more than the property is worth," Carla confided to Norma, her mother's friend.

"Insurance?" Norma asked.

"I haven't found anything about life insurance yet," Carla said. "I don't know what to do."

"Well, I know they had an attorney," Norma offered. "Gary Brown, I think his name is.

"Really?" Carla said hopefully.

Norma nodded. "Yeah, I think that's his name. Let's look it up in the phone book."

It was actually Garrett Braun, but Carla was thankful for the help. After the funerals were over, she made an appointment to talk with him.

"I'm real sorry to hear about them dying," the kindly man said. He reminded Carla of a teacher she once had. "They both had wills, you'll be happy to hear. Left everything to their only child. That would be you, I assume?"

"I have a brother, so what about him?" Carla asked in confusion.

"There's nothing about another child," he said. "It just names you, Carla."

"Well, my brother has been away for a very long time. I don't even know exactly where he is. Maybe Mom had his address somewhere." She shook her head. "I don't understand why Mom would cut him out of her life. That doesn't seem right."

"Well, let's go with the will and cross the bridge of your brother another time, shall we?"

"Yes, but was there anything of value? Any way I can pay for the house?"

"You could," he said. "But, do you want the house?"

"I don't know," Carla admitted. "So, what exactly am I looking at?"

"Well, it will take a few weeks to sort it all out, but I think there will be enough for you to pay off everything and still have something for yourself easy enough."

"I don't care as long as the debts get paid and I can get out from under this." Carla looked down at her hands. "Wait! Did you just say a few weeks?"

"Yes, probate is a slow process."

"I'll try to explain that to my aunt. She's not a very patient person." Carla was speaking more to herself than to the attorney.

"She's not in either will, so does that matter?" He asked.

"Oh, yes. It matters," Carla said ruefully. "Not to you so much, but this will all matter a lot to her."

Carla called Mary Maude again that night.

"You said you would call more often," Mary Maude whined.

"I've got so much to do to get all these finances straight," Carla answered.

"How much longer you gonna be gone now?"

"I'm not sure, but it may be a couple more weeks."

"Why?" Mary Maude demanded.

"It's just the way it is, Auntie Em. I've got to sell all their stuff and give away a bunch. I've got to work with the lawyer to clear the will. I'm trying to sell the house. There's so much to do."

"I suppose," Mary Maude conceded. "But we do need you back here. That Kaylee girl isn't working out. She's the laziest good for nothing I've ever seen."

"Auntie Em, she loved Jason. She's going to have his baby."

"Now, that's a fine excuse to be lazy," Mary Maude snorted.

"Well, be gentle with her and maybe she'll work out after all. I'll be home as soon as I can."

"You said home," Mary Maude observed.

"Yes. Yes, I did. I'll be home Auntie Em. I'll be home."

*　　*　　*　　*　　*

Sam did hire another man to help outside. His name was Phillip and he was almost as old as Sam, himself. But, he didn't mind climbing up on the roof or doing the hard work in the garden and yard.

"I'm gonna get rid of her," Mary Maude announced at dinner one night. Lester choked on his potato.

Sam frowned. "What you mean?"

"Just take her away, Sam. Back to town or something. I can do the work here just fine."

"When's Carla comin' back?" Sam asked. "What's takin' her so long anyway?"

"I don't know. She says it's about the wills or something. Guess Katie Jean and her husband had a bunch of debt. I think she's selling the house and their stuff, or something."

"Maybe, just maybe, she's not comin' back," Sam muttered.

"No, now Sam, she told me she'd come home. She actually said home. She'll be back, I know it."

"Hmmm," Sam said.

"S'cuse me folks," Lester got up and wandered outside, taking Phillip with him.

"He gonna work out?" Mary Maude asked.

"Think so," Sam answered.

"He's as old as you are," she observed.

"Well, he's willing and bull strong," Sam smiled.

"Can you find me another girl and take this one back, Sam?" Mary Maude pleaded.

"We'll see," he said. "We'll just see."

When Mary Maude heard a pig squealing in the early morning, she baked a cake and busied herself with laundry. She couldn't hear the noise from outside when she was down in the basement with the washer going. Later in the day, Sam came home with another girl. "This here is Bonnie," he said to Mary Maude. She was older than some of the girls they hired, but she seemed willing to work hard at keeping the house cleaned. Mary Maude had her clean up the extra bedroom upstairs, the one that Kaylee had slept in.

"Just throw all them clothes and stuff in that box," she pointed at a large box on the floor. "Sam will know what to do with it all. When you have the room cleaned out, you can have it for your own."

When Sam came in to get the box, he told Mary Maude that he'd slaughtered a pig that morning.

"Is that what all the noise was about?" She asked, eager to have a story for Carla when she came home.

"Yep, them hogs went kinda crazy with the blood smell."

"I heard them. I thought…"

"Now, Maudie." Sam soothed. "We won't talk about it. She's gone and that's all there is to it." He paused. "The pig's in the cooler. Lester and me will cut her up in the morning, I reckon. Get us some fresh side pork."

When Sam went back outside, Mary Maude hung out the wet clothes and checked on the new girl. She was done with the bedroom and was putting her own things away. "Guess I'm replacing somebody else, huh?" Bonnie ventured.

"You might say that," Mary Maude answered. "Hope you're not as lazy as she was."

"No, Ma'am, not me," said Bonnie. "I like a clean home and I'll enjoy helping you clean this beautiful old place."

"Don't you have a home of your own? I mean are you homeless, or what?"

Bonnie sighed and shook her head sadly. "No, I lost it all after my husband died and then my daughter, well, she died, too. I just kind of withdrew from life for awhile and when I got my shit together, there wasn't nothing left and I was livin' in my car. Pretty soon, I didn't even have a car..." she shrugged. "So, what can I start on? I surely like to clean."

"That's a good start," Mary Maude said. "Don't clean the room down at the end of the hall. That's my niece's room and I'll take care of it. She'll be home one of these days."

"Yes, Ma'am," Bonnie smiled. "So, what do you want me to do next then?"

Mary Maude showed Bonnie the chore chart she and Carla had made. "Just follow this chart," she said without much interest. Make sure to stay out of Carla's room, though."

"Carla is your niece?" Bonnie asked with interest.

Still, Mary Maude couldn't bring herself to like this girl/woman. *She's already trying to take Carla's place,* she told herself. "Yes, she'll be home soon then you and her can discuss how to share the chores."

"Okay then, I guess I'll just start with the kitchen." Bonnie began.

"No!" Mary Maude snapped. "I mean, I will take care of the kitchen today. You do the other stuff." Mary Maude waved at the chore chart and turned to clear up the countertop.

Bonnie looked at her new employer closely. *She's going to be hard to work for. She seems so sad. I wonder if the niece is alive at all. Maybe the girl died and she's just too sad to accept it. I've got to be real careful of her feelings.* With a short nod and her mouth held into a firm line, Bonnie got out cleaning supplies and began dusting the house, top to bottom. When that was done, she began to dustmop all of the hardwood floors. There were not many carpets, so this was a huge part of the work. She marveled at how clean the house was. "This is really easy work if done daily," she murmured. She was aware of Mary Maude checking on her once in a while. She didn't speak, just looked into the rooms where Bonnie was working, then went away.

When Mary Maude was done cleaning the kitchen, she walked outside with cold drinks for herself, Sam and Lester. She waved Sam to the patio, holding up a drink as enticement.

Sam stopped at the outside spigot to wash up his hands and arms. He yelled for Lester to take a break from cutting up the hog. Lester followed Sam's example and washed himself up before joining Mary Maude at the house. "Where's the girl?"

"She's in there, a-cleaning up a storm," Mary Maude said. "I left her a drink on the table."

"You don't like her much." Sam observed.

"Well, she's a worker and don't need no reminding." Mary Maude sighed. "Maybe I'll get used to it."

Sam didn't comment. He could see the sadness in his wife and didn't know how to reach her. She was pining away for Carla, that was evident. "Is she coming back?" He asked softly.

Mary Maude shrugged. "Said she was," she answered.

"What's takin' so long, I wonder?"

"Says it's complicated," Mary Maude almost whispered, as if she was talking more to herself than to him.

"She knows a lot about us, Maudie," he added.

She nodded. "That she does." She paused, then added, "well, if she was gonna do anything, I think we'd already know about it. It'll be all right."

She looked at Sam. *We're an odd pair,* she observed. *Sam's in his sixties already. It makes me feel old, too. Let's see, how old am I anyway? Well, pushing 45, I guess it is.* "That's not old!" She suddenly said aloud.

"What's that?" Sam looked bewildered.

"I'm not old," Mary Maude said in wonder.

Sam and Lester both stifled laughter. "Nobody said you was," Sam choked out.

"Well," she waved a hand at him. "I've been moping around here like I was older than dirt."

Sam couldn't hold his laughter. "Maudie, you're talkin' crazy."

Bonnie came wandering out of the house. "Is that my drink in there, Maude?"

"Mary Maude!" Mary Maude snapped. But, she couldn't hold her nasty tone. "Yes, it's your drink. Grab it and join us. I'm outnumbered out here."

"And get some for Phillip!" Hollered Sam. "He's done finished his job already and must've worked up a mighty thirst, I'm thinkin'."

Bonnie returned with a smile. She was introduced to Lester and Phillip, who was standing near the patio. She handed him one of the glasses of lemonade.

It was Sam who realized that Lester was eyeing the new girl. *Woman, I should say,* he thought. *She's more of an age for him, not much younger than Maude, I'd guess. I wonder…* "Lester," Sam prodded him with an elbow. "Why don't you show Miz Bonnie around? Maybe she'd like to see the gardens and the barn and all."

Lester turned instantly red. "Well, if you want," he looked shyly at Bonnie.

Bonnie smiled at him. "I'd like that," she answered. She boldly grabbed his arm and turned toward the garden.

"What're you doin'?" Mary Maude hissed at Sam.

"Watch and see," Sam answered. "You want some contented help, you watch them two settle together and work hard." Sam looked at Mary Maude and pulled a stray lock of her hair away from her face. "Just like you and me, Maudie," he said softly.

Mary Maude scoffed. She looked at Sam, then looked after the couple walking to the garden. "You think so, Sam?"

"Just you wait and see," he said.

After that event, Bonnie seemed to be everywhere at once. She finished her house chores and went outside to "spruce up things a bit." Mary Maude saw that Bonnie took good care of flowers and shrubs around the house, and she did some of the mowing, too. Sam and Lester expanded an old field by fencing it all in and they bought cattle. Phillip had some knowledge of cattle, he told them, and so this would be his job while Lester and Sam took care of the rest of the farm. There were some chickens that roosted in the barn and Bonnie was good at finding the eggs they laid.

"Why, it's become a regular little farm," Mary Maude said one night at dinner.

Sam seemed happier than he had ever been.

*   *   *   *   *

"Miss Mary Maude," Bonnie said one morning after breakfast dishes were done. "Me and Lester, well, we uh, we were thinking on getting hitched, you know." She looked closely at Mary Maude, then hurried on. "We were thinking, maybe we could fix up that loft over the garage and live there, if that's all right with you and Mister Sam, that is."

"Huh," Mary Maude responded. "Ain't that just something." She looked sternly at Bonnie. "Things would have to stay the same. I mean you would still have to work and all."

Bonnie beamed a smile. "Of course, that wouldn't change. We love it here, Ma'am."

"I just know I'll have to hire another helper," Mary Maude mumbled. "How does Sam think this is gonna work?" She turned abruptly away and walked outside. "Sam!" She yelled, beckoning him to come to her.

Sam was talking with Lester and Phillip out by the garage. "It's going to take a lot of fixing, Lester," he was saying. "We haven't used it for much of anything but storage for a long time. Most of what's in there belonged to Miz Maude's father. But, I'll talk to her…" He turned when he heard Mary Maude call his name. "Lordy, she knows already," he mumbled. Sam couldn't get a good read for his wife's mood as he walked toward her. *Half angry, half….no, don't let it be that.* He shook his head as he approached her. "What's happened?" He asked with dread in his voice.

"You told me and I didn't believe it," she stated. "That girl in there wants to marry Lester. What do we do now?"

Sam breathed a sigh of relief. *That's all,* he thought. "Well, and why not, Maudie?"

"I seen you over there talking with him. Is he of like mind, then?"

"Yep," Sam scratched the back of his balding head. "Wants to fix up the old garage and make an apartment up in the top."

"What's in that old garage?" She looked at the run-down building.

"Well, your Papa's old car and some tools. Mostly junk covered with years of dust and cobwebs."

"Does that old car even run?" She asked in awe.

"Don't know, Maudie. We've always used t'other one and the old farm truck."

"Is there anything valuable?"

He shook his head. "Don't reckon. I haven't even been in there in forever. Nothing I needed in there."

"Get me another girl for the house then, Sam. Somebody useful, not tiresome. Cause Bonnie is gonna be busy with her own place, I guess, and keeping up the outside." She paused to consider. "She's good at landscaping stuff, you know."

Sam smiled as he breathed a sigh of relief. "Yep, she's made the old place look right pretty. And," he added. "If they fix up that old garage as good as they do everything else, it will make this place look real good."

"Well, that may be so," she said with a hardened voice. "But, this place is mine and will always be mine. If anybody gets it, it will be Carla and nobody else. They ain't family and I don't like you treating them like they are."

"Now, Mary Maude," Sam began. She looked sharply at him because he almost never used her full name. "You're making too much of this. They deserve to be happy just like you and me. They're still the hired help on the farm here. And they're both good help. We don't want to lose good help." He paused and softened his voice. "And if Miss Carla comes back, you will have your daughter again. She's truly yours now that your sister's gone, I guess."

Tears sprang to Mary Maude's eyes. She looked at Sam through the blur and gave him a weak smile. "I hope that's true, Sam. I hope that's true."

He held her close to him then, and she let him, in a rare moment of tenderness. "It's all right, Maudie. It's all right.

She pushed away from him. "Go get me somebody I can bully, Sam. Just get me somebody that I can order around and get some satisfaction.

Bonnie ain't it and I can't get rid of her, it seems, either. You know I need somebody. Go." With that, she turned to the house and went to her room. She passed by Bonnie who was still in the kitchen, but didn't speak a word to her.

Sam sighed. "It won't never end," he whispered to himself. But, he got into the car and went to town. When he returned, he had a young girl who looked like she'd been dragged through the mud. She evidently hadn't bathed in a long time, but she was willing to work, she told him. Sam suspected she was an addict and would run away at the first chance, when she had a little money or something. She told him her name was Charity. He didn't believe her, but he went along with it. It wouldn't matter in the long run, he knew that.

"Charity?" Mary Maude scoffed. "What kind of a name is that?" She looked closely at the girl standing defiantly in front of her.

"I, uh, I don't know. Do you like Suzy better? It don't matter much to me."

"Huh!" Mary Maude responded. "Where'd you come from anyway?"

"Does it really matter to you? I thought you just wanted a maid or something." She sighed heavily. "Can I get some sleep? I mean, it's late and all, isn't it? I'll work tomorrow."

"You," Mary Maude pointed at the girl with a long, bony finger. "You will work when I tell you to work or you will be gone. Do you understand me?"

"Sure, you're the boss." The girl called Charity yawned in what appeared to be boredom. As she raised her arms above her head, Mary Maude could see the needle marks on her arms.

"So, you're a druggie, huh?" Mary Maude asked.

Charity quickly lowered her arms, pulling her sleeves down to her hands. "So, I used a little," she said.

Mary Maude turned toward the hallway leading to the kitchen. "Bonnie!" She yelled. "Bonnie, come and take this drug fiend to her room." Her voice lowered as Bonnie walked toward her. "She needs a bath and some sleep. Put a couple of water bottles next to her bed. She's gonna need them by morning." She started to turn away. "Oh, and she's also gonna need a puke bowl, I suppose."

Bonnie nodded and gently pushed the girl toward the stairs. "Up that way," she indicated with a nod of her head. She led the girl to an empty bedroom and showed her the bathroom. "Get cleaned up before you touch anything," she advised. "We keep a clean place here. Throw your clothes out here in the bedroom and I'll get rid of them. There are some clean things in the dresser and closet, so you can find something to fit you."

"What kind of place is this?" Charity whined. "That old broad is like some kind of witch or something. I don't think I can stay here." She was already getting the shakes of withdrawal. All she wanted to do was have one more hit and get some sleep. *Why did I come here? You know why, Stupid. You thought that old man just wanted to do you and maybe he'd give you some money and drop you off somewhere. You got yourself into a real mess now, didn't you?* She felt the stirrings of vomit rising to her throat. With a moan, she reached for the bowl that Bonnie left sitting on the dresser. *Oh, what the hell?* She thought. *maybe I can really get clean this time.* She looked at the room for the first time. At least it was clean, not like the rat hole she'd been staying in down by the railroad. She fumbled her way into the bathroom and drew a hot bath. "Haven't done this since I was a kid," she smiled ruefully. "If I die tonight, I'll go out clean on the outside anyway."

Bonnie picked up the dirty clothes and threw them into the garbage. She covered the naked girl on the bed and laid out a set of clothes for when she woke up. The bowl was full so she dumped it in the toilet, washed it out, and returned it to the bedside where she'd found it. Over the next three days, Charity went through the shakes, fever, and tremors over and over. She called out for someone named John and apologized over and over to her parents. At last, she settled into a quiet sleep. Bonnie changed the bed twice a day, rolling Charity over like a nurse does in the hospital. If truth be told, Charity reminded Bonnie of her own daughter who died of an overdose a few years ago. "I wonder how old you are, Charity," Bonnie whispered. "My Charity was only sixteen. I think you're a little older. Are you eighteen, maybe?" She used a wet cloth to wipe Charity's face, neck, and arms. "You'll be all right. Miz Mary Maude will take good care of you if you work hard and don't talk too much. You'll see. It will be all right. You can live here for the rest of your life, maybe."

"What are you doing?" Mary Maude demanded from the doorway.

Bonnie dropped the cloth. "Good gracious, Miz Mary Maude! You scared the bajeebers out of me!"

"Well, what are you doing?"

"I'm just nursing her back to health so she can get to work helping us."

"Hmmm, I wonder if she's gonna be much help at all."

"I'll see to it," Bonnie promised. "She'll be a good girl, I know she will."

Mary Maude frowned. "What's your interest in this drug addict?"

"She, uh, reminds me of my daughter," Bonnie teared up as she looked down at the girl. It surprised her to see that Charity was awake and staring at her. "Oh!" She said. "Hello, there."

Charity raised up on one arm. "Get away from me," she growled. "I am not your daughter and I don't need somebody taking care of me." She looked up at Mary Maude. "I'll get dressed and get out of your hair. It was a mistake, my coming here. Don't know what I was thinking."

Mary Maude glared at both Bonnie and Charity. "You'll get out of that bed and come downstairs for some food. Then we'll talk about what you can do. If you work out, then you got you a job. If not, we'll just get rid of you. My Sam is good at that." She shifted her focus. "Bonnie, you got other work to do."

"Yes, Ma'am," Bonnie scurried out of the room, inching past Mary Maude in the doorway.

"I don't want a job," Charity said. "I'll just get dressed and get out of here on my own. Your Sam doesn't need to be bothered about me."

"That isn't the way it works. You're here and you'll work. Is that understood?"

"What are you, crazy? You can't just keep me here like I'm a prisoner, you know."

"I'm trying to help you. Don't you want to be sober and have a life?"

"I have a life."

"Get dressed," Mary Maude went downstairs before the girl could say one more thing. *I'm glad I didn't have to raise any girl children,* she thought. *I couldn't handle this sassy talking back. I wonder if Carla was ever like this? Of course not! Carla was never an addict.*

Once Charity was good and clean, dressed decent, and combed out her hair, she was a pretty young girl. She also could see the benefits of working and living here in the house. The way Bonnie gushed over her made her feel special, if she let it, and she hadn't felt like that most of her life. Bonnie continued to nurse her to health and taught her to clean the upstairs. Bonnie still helped Mary Maude downstairs and helped Lester with the lawn and gardens. Phillip helped Sam with the farming, doing most of the work himself.

"There's clothes and stuff in that one bedroom," Charity remarked one day at lunch.

Mary Maude was incensed. "You stay out of that room, you hear?" She shouted.

"I thought I was supposed to clean upstairs, and that room was as dusty as everything!" Charity spouted back. "I thought you wanted everything spic and span."

"You watch your mouth when you talk to me," Mary Maude said menacingly. "That there room is none of your business. You stay out of there. I'll clean up in there if it needs it, not you." She turned on Bonnie. "Didn't you tell her to stay out of there?"

"I forgot. I'm sorry. I never even think of that room because I know you want to clean it yourself."

Mary Maude was mollified with the explanation. "That's settled then," she breathed, going back to eating her lunch.

"Yes, Ma'am," said Bonnie and Charity together.

Mary Maude inspected Charity's work and found it exceptional. She wasn't expecting that and it irritated her. She walked outside to cool herself off. Work was commencing on the garage and she was impressed with how quickly it was being done. "Who's that?" She pointed at some young men who were painting and building new window frames.

"Hired help," Sam said.

"What's this costing us?" She asked.

"A lot less than fixing the house up for a bed and breakfast that never happened."

"Hmpf," she snorted. "Keep them boys away from the house. I don't want that new girl to get distracted."

"They're staying out in the barn with Lester."

"How long?"

"A month, maybe."

Mary Maude walked into the opened garage and looked through some of Papa's old things. Sam had been right, most of it was covered with dust and cobwebs, and now there was a fresh layer of sawdust.

"That old car work?" A young man approached her. "I could use me a good old car like this one."

"No!" Mary Maude snapped. "You keep your thieving fingers off my Papa's car." With that, she turned and fled to the garden. She couldn't face going into the house and now the garage was off limits, too. "What's Sam thinkin', having those punks out here?" She fumed.

Sam watched her walk off. "It won't be long," he muttered.

"The Old Girl's in a mood, ain't she?" Lester commented. "Did I do wrong, wanting to fix this place up?"

"Don't disrespect her, Lester." Sam said. "No, it's getting harder for her to justify some things, you know? She's getting older. I think if Miss Carla would return, maybe things would be different. But, she's fighting her demons the best she can."

"Yes, Sir," Lester commented. "I gotta go look after the boys. Can't trust them alone for a minute."

"They ain't stealing stuff, are they?"

"Not yet," Lester called over his shoulder.

Sam walked to his wife. He didn't talk, just stood nearby, idly picking some weeds from the garden soil.

"I don't like it, Sam. There's too many."

"Not for long," Sam said back.

She looked sharply at him. "What you mean by that?"

"They're just short-term day labor. They won't be here long, just until the most of the project is done. I take them back to town in the evenin' and pick 'em up in the morning if-n they don't work so late they need to stay out there with Lester and Phillip."

Mary Maude nodded her head, but said nothing for a time. "You know something we never done?"

"What's that?"

"We never developed that old pond. We could maybe have an old boat out there, couldn't we?"

"I dunno, maybe. I'll have a look at it sometime."

"Is it very grown over?"

113

"Well, it's kinda marshy around the edges, but I never really explored it much. Old Jesse told me it wasn't much of a pond, even. Never wanted nobody out there, it seemed like."

"Oh. I always wondered about it, but never paid attention to it. I don't remember Papa ever going out there, either."

"Let's walk over there." He came closer and clasped her hand.

There were a lot of brambles that had grown up in the trees before they got to the wet ground. "Should've worn some boots," Mary Maude commented, holding tight to Sam's arm as she tried to find solid ground to walk on.

When Sam parted some reeds, they were both surprised at the size of the pond. It looked to be almost an acre or more of water surface, plus the marsh around it. "You know," Sam scratched his chin. "If we built a boardwalk around the marsh and a pier out into the water, I think you're right that we could have a rowboat or two out here."

"If Carla wants to open the B&B, this would be something for folks to do," Mary Maude breathed.

"Well, we'd have to fence off the sugar shack, though. Don't want no one going over there." He pointed behind them and to the right.

"You can't see it from here, Sam. People wouldn't even know."

"Well, people are nosey, so somebody would be snooping around it."

"I suppose you're right, then, so there's no sense in fixin' up the pond, either." She turned away in a huff as she picked a path back the way they'd come.

"I still think it's a good idea. I could take you out for a boat ride, maybe." Sam caught up to her and helped her pull a foot out of the ooze.

"Never mind, Sam," she growled. "It was a stupid idea anyway."

As they reached solid ground, Sam stopped and watched her walk away. Shaking his head, he looked at the path to the sugar shack. It was plainly visible from here. "I'll make a gate and fence it off," he determined. "And I'll get Lester and the boys out here to build us a nice boardwalk, too. She'll be happy about it when she feels better."

Sam and Lester walked around the pond and measured out where they wanted to put the boardwalk and the pier. Lester was almost as excited as Sam about the project. First things first, they built a chain link fence around the sugar shack and Sam locked the gate. The boys spent a couple of hours a day working on the pond project and the rest of the time finishing up the garage-apartment. Phillip talked non-stop about all the fishing he was going to do of an evening.

As they worked one day on the side nearest the sugar shack, Lester stopped the work and sent the boys to the garage early. "Sam, you come and look here," he said quietly. Down in the mud was a skull. It was old and was oozing with mud. Lester got a shovel and he and Lester dug around until they found more bones. They loaded them into the wheelbarrow. For days, they searched all around the pond, looking for any more bones that might have been there. All in all, there were four skulls and a lot of other bones. Sam and Lester dug a deep hole behind the sugar shack and dumped the bones in it. They covered them with lime and rocks, then filled in the hole.

"Must have been something Jesse done," Sam commented. "Maybe before he built the sugar shack, I'm thinkin'. Guess that's why he didn't want me around the pond. Huh."

"Well, it was stupid to put them in the water like that," Lester said.

"That's probably why he wouldn't let anybody out here near the water, I was sayin'. Always said it was haunted or somethin' like that. I never thought nothin' about it, but guess that's what happened, all right."

"Maybe it was haunted," Lester commented.

"Could be, I guess," Sam agreed. "This whole place is haunted one way or t'other, I'd say.

"It's took care of now," Lester said, wiping away the sweat from his face. "I don't want to clean up nothin' else, you know?"

"Me neither," Sam agreed.

"You gonna tell Mary Maude?"

Sam shook his head as he scratched his head behind his ears. "Nope, I don't reckon she needs to know about this. There's enough already."

Lester nodded his agreement and they put away the tractor and the tools.

A couple of days later, they resumed the work on the boardwalk. Sam wanted it finished before winter set in.

*　　*　　*　　*　　*

As it turned out, Charity had a flair for decorating. She and Bonnie started talking and Charity painted murals on some of the walls of the house and in the apartment that Bonnie and Lester were building. A month went by, and then another. She settled in with the routine of the house, even doing dishes and keeping up with laundry. Mary Maude was reluctantly impressed. But, she still felt uneasy around the girl. There was just something that she couldn't identify, something that kept her from trying to like the girl. It was almost as if she was familiar, somehow. "Does she look like somebody else I knew or something?" she pondered aloud. *I wish Carla was here,* she thought then. *I just want the peace she gave me, a purpose to live every day. I'm surrounded by people I don't even like.* She sighed heavily. *But, Sam does, it seems. He's happier than ever with all the outside projects and Lester and that Phillip-person to help him. And I have to admit, that Bonnie is about as handy as I used to be. I used to keep up with this whole house when I was younger.* Another sigh. *Who you fooling, Old Girl? You never did a lick of work when you were a girl. Mama saw to that. Ah, Mama, I surely do miss you.* She relived the moment once again when her mother reached for the falling wheelchair and fell herself, bumping over and over on the stairs until she lay dead at the bottom. "It was never supposed to be you, Mama," she whispered for the umpteenth time.

*   *   *   *   *

Sam announced a surprise just after lunch one fine, fall day. "Come with me, Maudie," he said. "I got a big surprise just for you."

"We got the house, Ma'am," Charity urged her on.

"Sure we can take over here for a minute," Bonnie chimed in. "You two go off and have a good time."

"Well, what the world?" Mary Maude looked confused.

"Just come with me," Sam stood and offered her a hand.

Mary Maude went with him out the back door, across the rose garden and toward the trees. As they approached the woods, she saw a new boardwalk along the edge of the swampy ground. It turned into the swamp and she lost sight of it. "When did you have time to do this?" She asked in awe.

"Oh, me and Lester and Phillip have been working on it, time to time, along with those boys getting' us a good start back in the summer. They cut out a lot of them brambles and swamp grass and such" Once again he moved a strand of her hair back behind her ear. "It sure helped to have Bonnie do the mowing and those boys to do the hard labor on the apartment and the garage, too." He laughed lightly. "Course, they more than helped us with this project, like I said. It was fun keeping this secret right under your nose."

"Well, I'll be," she breathed as they walked around the pond. As the water came into her view, she was awestruck. "It's truly beautiful, Sam. It really is. It's more than I ever imagined." She stopped to view the water and the ducks still lingering.

He put an arm around her and kept her walking to the pier that went out into the water. There were two rowboats tied to the pier.

"You don't aim to get me into one of them boats, do you?" She asked as she planted her feet and stopped.

He nodded. "I do. Come ride with me, Maudie."

"I don't want to fall into that dark water, Sam," she shuddered.

"You won't. I won't allow it."

She got into the boat and he rowed them around the pond as smoothly as though he'd been rowing a boat all his life. She sat unmoving for quite a while, but finally relaxed and began to enjoy the ride and watching Sam row smoothly through the water. It was relaxing to be out here, looking at the bushes and trees. At last, her gaze fell on the sugar shack. There was a new, chain link fence surrounding it, with a wide gate on the path. "It's locked up, then?" She nodded.

"Well, if we get strangers out here, we don't want them in that old building. It ain't safe, you know."

"It looks perfectly sound," she commented.

He laughed right out loud. "Well, but it ain't safe to have a bunch of strangers being nosey, you know."

"I suppose," she said quietly. "It wonders me that Papa never wanted anybody out here. It's a beautiful place. Did he ever tell you why, Sam?"

"He never did, you know," Sam answered truthfully. "It was part of his sugar shack area and he just kept people out of here, mostly."

"Except you," she said softly. "He shared everything with you. Why not this?"

Sam just shook his head, not meeting her eyes.

"What'd you find out here, Sam?" She asked. She began looking at the water. "This water is black as death, Sam." She commented.

"I reckon so, Maudie," he breathed. "I reckon so."

She nodded and became quiet with her thoughts about her father.

"Is Carla ever coming back?" Sam changed the subject, breaking into her thoughts.

"She says she thinks she will be finished with whatever is keeping her there by Christmas," Mary Maude smiled. "I hope that's true. I miss her something awful."

"Is this Charity girl working out?"

"Nope."

"I thought she was. Miss Bonnie is taken with her."

"Yeah, well I don't like her, you know."

"Who? Bonnie or Charity?"

"Well, truth is, I don't like either one of them. But, Bonnie is useful and her and Lester are kinda like family, I guess. At least, like family to you, I know. I can at least tolerate her and she works good."

"And?"

"And that girl is mouthy and stubborn. She's about outstayed her welcome, you know?"

"I'll take her back to town about Hallowe'en, I guess." Sam said in resignation.

Mary Maude smiled. "That's good. She's getting real tiresome."

"Yeah," Sam nodded as he pulled the boat up alongside the dock. "Hang on, I'll help you out."

They walked back to the house, hand in hand. Sam left her at the door and she went into the house humming the old tune she remembered her mother humming years ago.

Bonnie was amazed at the story about the pond. "Won't get me out there in no boat," she said. "I don't like water. Had me a cousin when I was a little girl who drowned. I remember them trying to revive him, but he just laid there." She shuddered at the memory. "Never did go near water again."

"That's the smell around here, then," Mary Maude tried not to smile.

"What smell?" Bonnie asked innocently.

Mary Maude laughed out loud. "You not goin' near water again," she said. "Maybe you should take a bath!"

Bonnie shook her head, half in bewilderment because Mary Maude had made a joke, and half at herself for not getting the joke. Charity laughed at them both.

A few days later, Charity was sent out to take a wheelbarrow load of old canned foods to the pigs. Mary Maude was cleaning out their food supply in the basement and emptied jars of food that had spoiled, or that she felt were too old to use anymore.

Sam watched the girl struggle with the load and then stand next to the fence, looking perplexed. "What you up to?" He asked.

Charity jumped at his voice. "Can't hear nothing with these pigs squealing like that," she explained her surprise.

Sam showed her how to dump the barrow between the boards of the fence, into the trough for the pigs to eat. It was gone in less than a minute.

"Wow, they was sure hungry," she commented.

"Pigs is always hungry," Sam replied.

"Mr. Sam, I was wondering. Did you ever hear of someone named Donna Sue?"

Sam stopped in his tracks, looking closely at the girl. "Don't reckon," he said slowly, rubbing his whiskery chin.

"Hm," she replied. "I just thought this might be where she worked a few years ago," she looked back at the house in thought. "But you don't think so?" She looked back at Sam.

"Nope," he said, shaking his head slowly. "What makes you think that?" He was fearful and curious. This was just a druggie he picked up off the street. How could she know about Donna Sue? *Have I got us into some kind of trap? Is this girl here to make trouble? How can that Donna Sue keep coming up time after time?*

"Well, my aunt was her mother and she used to tell everybody who'd listen this story about how her daughter just up and disappeared. Seems she worked on some farm or was a maid or something and I got to thinking it might have been here."

"Well, that's a story," Sam said, sweat running down his back, making it itch.

"Yeah, well, Aunt Jane was shipped off to the loony bin or someplace. But, after being here and getting to know Miz Maude, I just got to thinking."

"You got family to go home to, Girl?" Sam asked.

"Nah, like I told you, nobody wants me. Kinda like Donna Sue. She wrote me a letter once and said that her mom was already crazy and she was glad to be out of the house." She shrugged expressively. "I don't know, but from what she did say, it seems like she was here, you know?"

One slap with the shovel and she was over the fence with the pigs. She hardly made a sound as they went to work on her, but Sam wouldn't forget the look in her eyes as she lay face up in the mud. "Lester!" He shouted. "Lester, come help me!"

Lester and Bonnie both came running. Sam was trying to push the hogs off the girl, but they'd gotten some good bites.

"Oh My God!" Bonnie screamed. "I'll call 9-1-1."

"No, you won't!" Sam shouted at her as he and Lester pulled what was left of the girl out of the hog pen. "She's gone. Just leave it be."

"I think she has family, though…" Bonnie began before throwing up right there in the dirt.

Lester got the wheelbarrow situated so they could lay her in it. "I'll get the furnace started up," he nodded at Sam.

"No," Sam nodded toward Bonnie. "Get control of your woman. I'll take care of the furnace this time."

Bonnie was beside herself with grief. After a few days, Lester took her on a 'vacation' and they came back married. They moved into the apartment above the garage.

Mary Maude was content to greet Bonnie and get the routine back in order, but they were strained with one another. "Good thing she doesn't live here in the house," Mary Maude confided to Sam. "I can't stand the way she treats me, now."

"She was fond of the girl, Maudie. Can't fault her for havin' feelings."

"Well, she needs to get over it," Mary Maude said. After a moment's pause, she asked. "What happened? You were gonna take her back to town this weekend anyway."

"You were right about her, Maudie. She was bad news."

"S-a-a-m," she drawled. "What happened?"

"She was related to that Donna Sue-Girl," he said with a spit next to his lawn chair.

Mary Maude looked horrified. "How did that happen? How could you have been so clumsy as to get someone related to her?"

Don't know, rightly," he said with a sigh. "She was just standing on the street, kinda weaving around-like. You saw what shape she was in when she got here. I never did believe Charity was her name." He looked at Mary Maude with interest. "Did you?"

"I don't know." She replied crossly. "I'll make sure there's nothing left up there in her room."

"We already got rid of whatever she had, didn't we? Her clothes and all was pretty ratty."

"True," Mary Maude nodded. "But, I want to clean that room extra-good and burn anything she might have used or touched. Good riddance."

"Do you want I should get another girl for the house?"

Mary Maude smiled. "Nope. Carla is coming home soon. I'll just work extra hard until she gets here. I already cleaned up the bedroom real nice for her."

"Well, that's fine, then," Sam said with a smile. "How do you know?"

"She called again. She'll be home for Christmas, for sure! Probably before that." Mary Maude couldn't hide her smile.

They both saw the white plume of smoke from the sugar shack as it rose into the evening sky. Neither of them said anything, they just watched in silence, each caught up in their own thoughts.

They spent the night together in Mary Maude's bedroom. It was a rare occasion for Sam to still be in her bed in the morning. "Why do we have separate rooms?" She asked him when he got up.

He looked at her strangely. "That's how you always wanted it, I reckon."

"Well, it's silly of me, isn't it?" She said.

"If you say so, Maudie," he ventured cautiously.

"Me and Bonnie will move your things in here," she announced. "It doesn't make a lick of sense for me to have all this room and you to have your own room. I got this here queen-sized bed and a huge closet. Well, it just is silly. You come stay with me, Sam, won't you?"

"After all these years, Maudie?" He chuckled as he crawled across the bed and grasped her hand. "I never once thought you'd want me in here full-time."

"Do you love me, Sam?" Mary Maude asked almost shyly.

"I reckon I do, Maudie. I reckon I do."

She nodded. "My Mama is the only person who ever loved me," she whispered. "But now, I got both you and Carla. I don't know what to do with love." She bit at her lower lip.

"Your Papa loved you, you know." He ventured. "He was scared of you sometimes, but I do believe he loved you, too."

She pushed him away. "Nope," she said. "He loved Katie Jean. And there was a nanny I think he might have had an affair with once," she was looking thoughtfully at a picture of her parents hanging on the wall above her fireplace.

"Jesse?" Sam asked. "I'd never have thought that about him."

"Well, I don't know for sure, but I think so. Mama did, too." She stared at the picture. "You know what, though? I don't think Mama cared. They weren't very close, Mama and Papa. She, well she was hard to please. But, she loved me to distraction. I really was a spoiled little brat, I suppose. Anything I wanted she got for me somehow, and then anything I didn't want, she got rid of."

"And your Papa had Katie Jean," Sam said slowly.

"Yeah, kinda like his and hers kids, we were," she chuckled. With a kick of the covers, she jumped up. "Yep, you move in here and we'll have us another room for Carla's B&B, now won't we?" She twirled around before reaching for her robe. "This way, we can have a separate living room downstairs too, instead of moving us down there. I like it this way much better."

Sam shook his head and smiled after her retreating figure, as she walked into the bathroom.

CHAPTER NINE

Finally, Carla was coming home on Thanksgiving Day, for sure. Mary Maude was more excited than she had ever been. She and Bonnie cooked a great feast and set out the finest dishes in the dining room.

"Well, I can hardly wait to get to know the famous Carla," Bonnie ventured.

Mary Maude stopped for a moment to consider. "Well, I guess you never got to be around her at all, did you?"

"Can't remember if I did or not, truth to tell. Too much has happened since she was here last."

Mary Maude knew Bonnie was referring to the girl, Charity. It made her angry that Bonnie still moped around about the girl. "Why'd you like her so much anyway?" She asked without realizing she was speaking it out loud.

"Didn't really know her, I said," Bonnie looked confused.

"No, no, no, I mean that Charity-Girl."

Immediately, Bonnie teared up. "I had a girl once," she wiped at her eyes, her voice husky with emotion. "Her name was Charity, too. And she died of an overdose, too many years ago to think about now. This was like reliving that time, you know, when Charity came here she was so strung out. It just melted my heart."

"I didn't know," Mary Maude said quietly. "Did Sam know this?"

Bonnie shook her head. "No, I only told Lester while we were off on our little holiday." She smiled weakly, grabbing a tissue to blow her nose.

"So, there's no connection?" Mary Maude asked. "I mean, like, she wasn't related to you or anything?"

"Who?" Bonnie looked completely confused. "Oh, the girl who… you mean, Charity?" Bonnie shook her head again. "No, no, I never saw her until she showed up here. Why did you think I might be related to her?"

Mary Maude shrugged. "I don't know. Well, you just seemed so taken with her…" She shrugged again.

"Honey, are you all right?" Bonnie looked genuinely concerned.

"What did you just call me?"

"I'm sorry, Mary Maude. I know you're a very private person. But, I do feel we have built some kind of friendship, don't you?"

Mary Maude abruptly turned to walk away. "I don't know," she said under her breath. "Don't talk to me."

Later, Bonnie talked quietly to Lester in their loft home. "Why didn't they want to call the police, Lester? It just isn't right what they do."

"It's their way." He said into the darkness. "They're not bad people, Bonnie. They just got into a habit, I guess. It isn't like people is busting down the door to talk to her, you know. Seems like nobody misses her." *Or many another,* He thought to himself.

"It's just so sad. I feel like we could get in some kind of trouble, you know? We live here, too."

"I been here quite a spell and there's never been no trouble that I know of." He paused as if thinking. "Well, there was one family that came and asked about some girl, but she run off, so we didn't know anything about her anyway."

"You're sure she ran away?" Bonnie asked with suspicion in her voice.

"Now, don't go making trouble. We got us a good gig here. I was down and out, homeless and livin' on the streets. You wasn't much better. We got it good now. Let's not make trouble, you know?"

"I 'spose," she murmured before drifting off to sleep.

During the night, Sam was spreading ashes over the flowers. It would be good fertilizer for the spring when everything bloomed again. Mary Maude joined him. "That the last of it?" She asked.

"What you doin' out here?" He asked. "You don't even have a coat."

"Why do you keep them hogs, Sam?" She asked.

"Pigs, cows, chickens, ducks; it's all food, Maudie. You know that."

"I reckon I do," she sighed as she walked away. "I reckon we're as normal as other folks, in the end."

"Tomorrow's a big day!" He called after her.

She only waved a hand to let him know she had heard him.

*　　*　　*　　*　　*

Mary Maude was amazed at the moving truck that pulled into their driveway. And more amazing than that was that Carla was driving it. Her car was hooked up at the back. She parked the truck and ran lightly over the lawn to fall into Mary Maude's outstretched arms. "I'm home," she breathed.

"Oh, Girl, I can hardly believe it!" Mary Maude was laughing and crying all at the same time. "It took forever!"

"I know," Carla broke away. "Is dinner ready?"

"You know it is!" Mary Maude boomed. Her loud voice echoed through the house. It was a signal for Bonnie to poor drinks at the table.

There was so much catching up to do. Everyone talked at once, trying to fill Carla in on what all had happened. "You got married?" Carla exclaimed, looking first at Bonnie and then at Lester.

"Yeah, we did," Lester spoke first.

Bonnie was nodding happily. "We fixed up the old garage and we live out there now."

"Really?" Carla looked at her aunt. "You let them live out there? That's great news. You won't get so lonely and yet they have their own space. It's perfect."

"Well," Mary Maude said. "It's perfect now because my girl came home. I've missed you something fierce."

"I've missed you, too, Auntie Em," Carla grabbed her aunt's hand. "And, I've brought a bunch of furniture, lawn furniture and stuff for the house. I hope you don't mind. I think some of it actually came from here. It might have been family heirlooms or something."

Mary Maude frowned. "Other than the things from her bedroom, I don't think Katie Jean took anything else from the house."

"She once told me that some of the old furniture she had was from here. She said that your father brought her stuff from the attic or basement, or somewhere. Anyway, I've brought it all back." She beamed at everyone at the table.

"That's fine, Dear," Mary Maude said, but everyone could tell that she really didn't think it was fine at all. For some reason, the news seemed to upset her.

"I also have money to put into the place, if you want to. They had a good insurance policy. Are we still planning the B&B?" Carla asked. "I thought you and I could decorate the place together, give it an antique flavor, you know?"

Mary Maude smiled slowly. "You're right," she nodded. "It will be all okay. You'll see to that. Won't she, Mister Sam?"

Sam looked up from his plate with a smile. "I reckon," he nodded. "Things ought to get right settled down here now. I ain't for certain about having strangers, but I guess you women-folk will take care of all that." He pointed with his fork. "Me and Lester will just stay outen your way."

Lester nodded. "That's for sure," he mumbled into his food.

"Sam," Carla began slowly. "I was wondering if we could bury my folks out there in the garden near my mom's parents?"

"What?" Mary Maude looked alarmed. "You brought their bodies out here?"

Carla tried not to laugh. "No," she shook her head. "I brought their urns with ashes in them. I just thought it would be fitting for us all to be here on this farm. Is that okay?"

Sam had stopped eating, and looked at her with something that appeared to be respect. "Did it up right proper, did you?" He asked, looking at Mary Maude.

Carla nodded with a sigh. "Yeah. It was a lot of hassle, paperwork, and emotions." She couldn't keep the tears from falling.

"Well, Maudie?" Sam looked at his wife, his head tilted back. "What you think about that?"

"To have Katie Jean right here," Mary Maude said quietly. She looked at Sam and they stared at one another for a few seconds. "I reckon it's okay, Sam," she said with a sigh, nodding her head. Turning to Carla, she added. "You ended up my girl anyway. Sure, bury them out there. It won't hurt nothing."

When the women were gathered in the kitchen to clean the dishes, Carla gave them another surprise. "There is one more thing, Auntie Em," she said.

"Oh? What's that?" Mary Maude kept washing the dishes.

Carla took a big breath. "That would be Andrew."

Mary Maude turned to look at her. "What?"

"Well, it seems we just were spending a lot of time together because he works at the funeral home, and well, we went to school together, so we've known each other forever. And, well, we kind of got engaged about a week before I came home." Carla held up her left hand where a diamond sparkled in the light.

"No!" Mary Maude turned from the sink, water dripping on the floor. "No, I won't allow it! You can't keep bringing more and more people into this house! You know how I am! How could you do something like this to me?" She fled for the garden.

Carla started after her, but Bonnie stopped her. "Leave her be, Carla," she said. "Mister Sam will take care of it. He's the only one who can." Bonnie paused. "She'll come around," she said. "She did for me and Lester, after all, and you are family. She'll come around."

"I knew she'd be upset. But, I mean, well, he isn't gonna move out here right away or anything. He's still got school to finish and he's a part owner of the funeral home. He can't up and leave." Carla was crying softly, so she turned and fled to her room, leaving Bonnie with the clean up. She put her clothes away with a vengeance, anger building up as she worked. *She can't just expect me to never want to have a life of my own!* She fumed. *I am free, independent and well over 21 now! Andrew would be such an asset to this place and I would have someone of my own. She has Sam, and Bonnie has Lester. What does she expect?*

When Carla came out of the bathroom a few minutes later, she was only half-surprised to see her aunt standing near the window beside her dresser, looking outside. Carla stopped in the doorway, her hand still on the knob. *If this goes south, I'll just lock myself in the bathroom,* she decided. But, she didn't speak. She just waited.

"When I was your age, I never thought about a man in my life. I just accepted my life here on the farm and that was that. One day, I looked up at the table and there sat Sam. It just seemed like a good idea to marry him. Papa trusted him. He already knew all about the farm and he was willing. He never hesitated, just up and went to the church with me and we got married. That's all there was to it." Mary Maude sighed deeply. "I don't know exactly when I knew I loved that old man, but I do. I can't even imagine now what I would do without watching him from the windows and having him to talk me out of my crazy notions, you know?" Mary Maude turned to smile weakly at Carla.

Carla nodded, but remained quiet. She walked to the bed and sat down.

127

Mary Maude turned back to the window. "I want things the way I want them, Carla. I don't like to share, and I don't like people very much. I get tired of people real easy. Papa always was here to take care of that, ever since I was a girl. Sam, well Sam is a lot like Papa. He always takes care of me, talks me down, is there when I need…." She just stopped talking, still looking out the window, one hand on the curtain, her fingers running along the edge.

"I know," Carla said softly. "I love Andrew, Auntie Em. He's going to come to visit a few times so you and Sam can get used to him, to us together." She breathed deeply and let her breath out slowly. "I'm not going to leave you ever again. I'm here to stay and I hope that you can accept Andrew someday."

Mary Maude turned quickly to look at Carla. "I never wanted a house full of people. I never thought I would have to entertain strangers. It's all I can do to have girls here to work for me. They get so tiresome and I can get rid of them, send them away. I can't do this. What do I do when I can't stand it, when it gets… when it gets tiresome?"

"So, we don't start up the B&B then," Carla said with a shrug.

"That's not what I mean."

"Well, what then?"

"I don't like people taking up space in my house and being underfoot when I don't want them there."

"What about Lester and Bonnie?" Carla asked.

"They don't live here in the house. Didn't you see they fixed up the old garage and live out there?"

Carla hung her head. "Sorry, I forgot. I just got here today, Auntie Em."

"I'm sorry, too," Mary Maude answered. "I need to get used to change. I can't just accept it like some people." She walked to the door. "Where do you think you would live?"

"I love this house. I want to live here forever."

"This here room isn't big enough for two. Move down the hall there to Sam's old room, why don't 'cha?"

Carla frowned deeply. "Sam's old room? Where's Sam sleeping, downstairs already? I didn't notice you'd changed the living room into a bedroom, yet."

Mary Maude snorted into a laugh. "He's staying in my room now, right up here." A broad smile crossed her face.

Carla raised her eyebrows in surprise. "Really?" She asked. "You let him move in with you?"

"Just seemed reasonable," Mary Maude answered as she walked out the door. "Gives us an extra room. Still does, if you move to his old room."

"Well, I'll be," Carla muttered. "Isn't that just something?"

*   *   *   *   *

The winter was a quiet one. They kept the house clean and played board games in the evening. Bonnie taught everyone to play Euchre, Bridge and Cribbage. Andrew came to visit on Tuesdays or Wednesdays every week. The first dinner together was awkward because Mary Maude stared at Andrew and questioned him like he was a teenager, dating her daughter. After that meeting, Andrew almost always found something for he and Carla to do, away from the house. Carla wanted to share her plans with him, so she showed him the bedrooms that she wanted to make into a Bed and Breakfast business, but Andrew acted as though he wasn't very interested. After the Holidays, Carla wanted to spend more time at the farm, but Andrew kept insisting on going out somewhere, anywhere, away from the farm. One day, to humor her, Andrew agreed to walk around the lake on the boardwalk.

"I don't know when Sam built this, but I'm glad he did," she clung onto Andrew's arm as they slipped and slid their way through the snow around the lake. "Maybe we can skate sometime, too. The pond is so inviting."

Andrew shook his head. "I'm not stepping foot on frozen water with all that liquid water underneath it."

Carla laughed. "It's safe, Andrew. I've skated a lot of times, and the pond isn't very deep in most places, Lester says."

"I've skated, too," he answered. "On a rink of completely frozen water sprayed over a cement base or something else solid. I will not step onto a lake with a skim of ice."

"A skim that's six to twelve inches thick," she laughed again. "And this little pond is hardly a lake."

They walked other times, but Andrew wasn't happy about the activity. One day Andrew asked about the sugar shack. "What is that old building?"

He pointed through the trees, beyond the fence, rubbing his gloved hands together and pulling up his collar against the cold breeze.

"It's a sugar shack," she answered quietly.

"Not many maples around here. Do they try to make their own syrup then?"

"No," she shook her head. "No, they don't use it anymore. That's why it's all fenced off, to keep people out of there."

He took a few steps closer to the chain link fence. "It looks to be in pretty good shape for an abandoned building. Too bad to let a building go like that, if that's what they're doing." He looked back at her with a frown. "Are you sure someone isn't using that building for something else?"

Carla pulled him back to the path, fearful that he would get closer and look into the windows. *I'll ask Sam to get film or something for the windows so people can't snoop,* she thought. "No, Andrew, they maybe store some old stuff in there, but it isn't being used. Let's go back to the house." She said. "I'm getting cold, and Sam really doesn't want anyone in his old buildings out here on the farm." She couldn't suppress the shudder that came over her.

"Yeah, and that explains the tracks in the snow, Carla," Andrew chuckled. "He is a strange duck, that Sam. As a matter of fact, the old girl is pretty weird herself. Are you sure they are related to you? You seemed so normal back at home. Even when we were in school, you seemed mostly normal. Not anything like these people."

Carla stopped right where she was. "What are you saying? Seemed so normal? You think I'm weird now, too?"

"I don't know. You just seem real, uh, different here."

"What do you mean?"

Andrew acted like he'd been caught with his hand in the cookie jar or something. He stamped his feet and rubbed his hands together. "You just lied to me for one thing. That building is being used. So, okay, maybe it is a storage shed now, I don't know. But those tracks were made after the first snow and probably a couple of times since." He looked like a defiant, little boy, his feet planted and his arms crossed.

How long has it been since we've held hands or since he's held me close? He looks like a little boy who's about to confess to a lie himself, or something.

"Well," he began in a pained voice when she didn't respond to him. "I really thought the B&B was just a dream thing, you know. I never thought you meant it. I mean, you seemed to have it altogether, but out here on this old place, you really are just a country girl with a plan for something that isn't going to work because your family is too strange for anybody to come here. It's an old place, Carla." He spread his arms out to include the house just visible from the trees where they were standing. "It reeks of something weird, or, hell, I don't know, just not a business opportunity." He shrugged, suddenly looking toward the house carefully. "And there's the old lady spying on us from that window up there. Now, tell me that's not creepy." He looked around them, suddenly pointing toward the barn. "And look at that!" He exclaimed. "There's the old man and his lackey watching us from the barn. Look, Carla. The old man is there by the door, and the other guy is up there in the loft. I can't do this," he began shaking his head. "I'm not a kid, you're not a kid. What are they waiting for, me to drop dead or to do something to you? That is just too, well, weird, for lack of a better word." He blew on his gloved hands. "Why don't you come back to the city with me and leave this to them? You aren't like them, you know, except when you're out here. I'm leaving. Come with me."

Tears sprang from her eyes, pouring down her face. Without another word, she turned and fled to the house. Andrew didn't follow her. Instead, he walked to the garage where he'd parked his car, got into it, and drove away.

Carla watched from a window, tears still streaming down her face. She looked at the ring on her finger, slowly twisting it round and round. It slipped off and before she could catch it, the ring fell to the floor, rolled to the furnace grate and dropped in with a hollow clink and clunk as it went into the pipes. "Well, I guess that's that," she muttered. Her sobbing had stopped, she realized.

"He coming back?" Mary Maude asked from the doorway.

Carla shook her head. "No, I don't think so." She looked up and gave a half-smile. "He thinks we're weird," she cocked her head to one side, raising the opposite eyebrow.

Mary Maude laughed. Carla listened to the husky voice as Mary Maude went down the hallway.

"Are we weird?" She asked her bedroom. "Am I different here? Why did he say something about dying?" As she idly arranged items on her dresser, she thought about her life here on the farm. *You know weird, even*

131

crazy things have happened here, she told herself silently. *But, when I'm here, Auntie Em doesn't do those things, does she? No, of course not. It's never happened while I was here, that I know of. But what about all that time you were gone,* her inner voice asked. *What happened while you were taking care of your parents and selling the house and all that?* Carla shook her head, refusing to think about it anymore.

However, when she and Bonnie were alone one day, she asked her. "Bonnie, while I was gone, did you have to take care of the whole house by yourself?"

"Oh, no," Bonnie said. "There was a couple of girls, I think." She moved closer to whisper. "One of them died right here in the house." She shook her head. "Wouldn't call 9-1-1 or nothing. Just took care of it, so they said. Lester wouldn't talk about it."

"Did they butcher a hog about that time?" Carla asked in dismay.

"Why, I believe they did, you know." She paused in thought. "Then, the t'other one, well she fell into that hog pen. It was awful what them hogs did to her."

Carla felt sick. It was just as she thought. When she was at the farm, nothing happened, but if she was gone, there was no telling what might happen.

Bonnie went on talking. "One of them, that girl that fell into the hog pen, I think. Well, she was asking a lot of nosy questions. She asked me about someone else who used to work here. I heard Miz Maude and Mister Sam talking about her being a cousin or something of a girl named, let's see, Debby or, Diana, no it was Donna Sue, I believe it was, anyway." Bonnie had stopped dust mopping and was standing in thought, her chin resting on her hand that held the mop.

"That's strange," Carla said aloud. She thought about the diary she'd found. Ellie wrote about Donna Sue. *Wasn't that who wrote the extra pages hidden in the closet? Was this new girl here to make trouble?. It sounded like Sam and Auntie Em believed that.*

"What you thinking, Girl?" Bonnie asked. "What you mean about it being strange?"

Carla shook her head. "There was a girl a long time ago, named Donna Sue. She ran away, I think. Her family came here and asked about her, but she was gone by then."

"Huh, well Charity came here as a drug addict. Mr. Sam found her down there with those bums by the railroad, I think." Sudden tears sprang to Bonnie's eyes. "I nursed her to health only to have that accident happen." She whispered again. "I think they cremated her out there in that old shack." A pause. "You ever been out there? I think they cremated Miz Maude's parents there, too. They're buried out there in the roses. Tch-tch-tch," she shook her head and went back to work.

Carla looked out a window in the room. *This is what Auntie Em does,* she thought. *now, here I am, staring out toward the barn, wondering what goes on out there. Surely, they do not kill anyone.* She closed her eyes, leaning against the cool glass. *I hoped it was all far in the past, that they don't kill anyone, and that it's just a bunch of stupid accidents. But, how many accidents can happen in one house, to one couple?* She looked up as movement caught her eye. She watched Lester walking from the barn to the house. *Does he know? Does he help Sam? It doesn't seem like Bonnie knows anything except what the sugar shack is really used for. But, what about Lester?* Carla rubbed her temples, a headache beginning to form. *Grandpa taught Sam and Sam must be passing it on to Lester. When will it end?*

"You feeling all right?" Mary Maude said from behind her.

Andrew's right, Carla thought. *She's always watching everyone. She always pops up when I think I'm alone.* A chill made her shudder. "I'm just tired, I think." She responded.

"Coming down with a cold or something?"

"No, I don't think so, just ready for spring and warmer weather." When Carla turned toward the door, no one was there. She frowned. *Was she really there? Was I just talking to myself?* But, no, she could hear Mary Maude walking slowly down the hallway and then down the stairs. "Maybe I'm going crazy," she muttered.

*   *   *   *   *

Spring, when it came, brought rain, sun, and wind. Bouquets of lilacs got placed on the tables and dressers in the bedrooms, adding their sweet aroma throughout the house. Mary Maude threw open every window possible to air out the house. "Too much stale air from the winter in here," she explained.

The work of the farm began in earnest. Plans for the vegetable garden and for a field of corn were laid. Sam and Lester talked about selling some of the animals and what ones they would butcher in the fall.

"What about the Bed and Breakfast?" Bonnie asked. "Are we gonna do that this year?"

"What do you think, Carla?" Mary Maude asked.

"Sure," she said. "I'm game. I'll get on the computer and make some fliers and put some ads out there. Let's see what kind of response we get."

"Do we need to hire another maid?" Bonnie asked innocently.

"No!" Carla and Mary Maude said together. They looked at one another sheepishly.

"Well, I usually help with the mowing and the flowers, and stuff," Bonnie added. "Who's gonna help around the house? Miss Carla can't do everything all by herself."

"True," Carla shrugged.

"Sam," Mary Maude looked at her husband. "Can you find another girl?"

Carla began shaking her head. "No, no I'll get someone. I can advertise for good day help. We need the rooms for paying guests, so we don't need anybody else living here with us, do we?"

Mary Maude looked closely at her niece. "What's that mean, day help?"

"Just someone who comes in to make beds and clean in the mornings then goes home every day."

"We always make living here part of the help's pay," Mary Maude began.

"Well, we'll be charging people for staying here, so their pay can come out of that income," Carla said in her practical way.

"I think Carla's got a good plan," Sam said. He was sweating profusely and wiped his handkerchief over his face.

"You feel okay, Sam?" Carla asked.

"Not feeling the best, I guess," he answered. "But, Maudie you should consider what the girl's saying. She's smart, you know." He stood up and announced. "I think I'll just sit awhile in my recliner there in the living room."

Mary Maude frowned, but didn't say anything. She watched him shuffle his way out of the dining room. "Go ahead and start whatever needs done outside, Lester."

"Yes, Ma'am," he nodded.

"I'll go out and help him," Bonnie added.

When they left the room, Mary Maude looked at Carla. "Day help, huh?" She asked. "We have to pay them and then they get to go home every day?"

"Yes," Carla said. "They come in the morning and help out, then they go home. Is that going to be okay with you? They won't be staying, maybe won't get too tiresome for you."

Mary Maude smiled slowly. "You handling me, Girl?" She asked.

"Maybe," Carla said with a smile. "But, it's for the best."

"Huh," Mary Maude got up and went outside.

Carla went to the computer to begin all the work to set up the business and get some advertising out. She spent days developing brochures and forms, going to the print shop to have them printed professionally. Carla dragged Mary Maude to the courthouse to file the proper documents for a business license and have inspectors come to the house. Sam took Mary Maude out for a drive when the inspectors were at the buildings, so she wasn't anxious and interfering with what needed to be done. There were only a few things that needed to be fixed. Carla hired a plumber and an electrician to make the repairs. Again, Mary Maude had to be distracted from "having strangers" in her home.

How is this even going to work? Carla talked in her head. *How is she going to put up with guests staying overnight, being in the house for breakfast, wandering around the lawn, flowerbed, and around the lake? Maybe this is all a mistake. What was I thinking? Auntie Em can't do this. Why is she letting me try?*

They planned to open the B&B on the last Monday of June. There was a carnival going on in town and it seemed like a good time to open up. Mary Maude wouldn't agree to a Grand Opening or an Open House, so Carla just put out fliers and ads in the local paper. She also included a color advertisement in a regional vacation booklet. A large sign was put out by the road announcing the business to passersby. "Aunt Em's B&B," it stated in bold letters with flowers around the edges. "A Taste of the Past". The wait was on.

Carla became worried about Sam over the next few days. He was sleeping more and more, leaving the outside work to Lester and Bonnie. When Sam was active, he seemed lethargic, uninterested in what was going on. The day before the B&B was to open, he didn't get up at all. "Where's Sam?" Carla asked at breakfast.

"He stayed in bed this morning," Mary Maude said. "He didn't even answer me when I tried to wake him up."

Carla was alarmed. "Let's try to get him up," she suggested.

"What for?"

"I'm worried about him. He's been dragging around here for weeks, not eating, not interested in anything. It isn't like him."

Mary Maude snorted. "Well, you can go try if you want to, but I'm telling you, he is dead to the world."

"That's what I'm afraid of," Carla said as she walked to the stairs.

And it was true. Sam had evidently died sometime during the night. His body was stiff and cold. Carla called for Lester and Mary Maude. After looking at the body and being sure he was dead, Mary Maude called a conference about what to do. "We just buried Papa in the garden, so I guess that's what we'll do with Mister Sam, too," she said. There was no emotion. Mary Maude was quiet and didn't cry or give any sign of her grief.

"We should call the coroner," offered Bonnie.

"No!" Mary Maude said sternly. "We don't need no strangers here prying into our business."

"Well, the man is dead and there needs to be some kind of official…"

"No!" Mary Maude said again. She looked pointedly at Bonnie, her eyes blazing, but her voice quiet and cold. "Lester, fire up the old furnace and do what needs to be done," she said without taking her eyes from Bonnie's face. "When it's done, we'll bury the remains right there beside our baby boys." She turned her gaze on Carla. "Where'd you put your parents?"

"Uh, they're next to Grandpa."

Mary Maude nodded. "Good, then put Sam next to the boys, like I said.

"Yes, Ma'am," Lester nodded and turned to go.

Bonnie followed him out the door. Carla and Mary Maude could hear her griping at him all the way down the stairs.

Mary Maude walked to the bed and looked down at her husband. "Good-bye, Sam," she said. "I wish you didn't die in my bed." With that, she walked out, clomping down the stairs.

Carla was left with the body. "There's nothing wrong with this," she said softly. "It's what he would have wanted. It's what they do. Why do I feel like there's something wrong?" She sighed, turning to walk out the door. "Oh, Lord!" She exclaimed. "We're supposed to open tomorrow!"

CHAPTER TEN

Nobody came to the B&B during the festival or for a month afterward. They watched the city fireworks from the front porch on the Fourth of July, but nobody came to stay. It was a relief to Carla because there had been smoke from the furnace on opening day, and she didn't want to have to explain that to anybody.

Mary Maude was moody, but quiet. Carla knew her aunt must surely be missing Sam.

At last, in August, they got a reservation. It was from a couple who were on their honeymoon and wanted a nice, quiet place to stay for two nights. It seems they had relatives in the area, but didn't want to stay with them.

Mary Maude had their breakfast ready the first day and was quick to tell them about the pond and boats, if they were interested. They paid extra for the boat ride, which they said was 'very romantic.' Mary Maude was pleased that this was a success and did her best to have their breakfast ready the second day. But, Carla could tell that she was ready for them to leave. They gave a good review online which pleased Carla, too.

"We can do this," Carla said at supper. "It went well."

"They stayed too long," Mary Maude whined.

"Only two days, Auntie Em," Carla replied.

"Yep, two days is too long."

"What if someone wants to stay a week?" Bonnie asked.

"That ain't happenin'," Mary Maude said.

"It could," Carla muttered.

"Not while I'm alive," Mary Maude scooted her chair back and left the table.

Carla watched her go.

"What you gonna do?" Bonnie asked.

"Nothing," Carla replied. "It will be fine."

"If you say so," Bonnie began gathering up the dishes. "You know, it puzzles me why people want to go out on that little pond in those flimsy boats." She shook herself and continued cleaning up the table before taking the dishes to the kitchen.

"You don't like boats?" Carla asked.

"I don't like water. Never learned to swim and never plan to." The swinging kitchen door closed between them.

Carla stood up to help her, taking a stack of cups to the kitchen. *What did you expect,* she thought. *You knew it wouldn't be easy. She spent years getting rid of people and you want to push them on her, in her own home.* "Ahhhhhhhhhhhh!" she sighed.

So, Carla didn't advertise as much as she could have. She couldn't take back what was already out there, but she didn't develop anything else. Mary Maude ignored everybody for two days, staying long hours in her own bedroom or walking outside in the gardens. She didn't walk around the lake, just kept herself near the house.

"You're lonely, Old Woman," Mary Maude looked around to see who was talking. She was quite alone. "I must be goin' crazy," she muttered. She knelt on the ground near the graves of her family. "Hm-m-m-m," she moaned, rolling off her knees to sit on her bottom. "Well, Sam, I don't know if I can do it," she said.

She heard the voice again. "I told you not to do it."

Mary Maude nodded. "I know you did," she whispered, tears beginning to stream down her face. "I just thought it would be okay because they wouldn't be staying long, you know? I should have listened to you, Sam." She shook her head, her fingers busily cleaning weeds that were threatening to cover the graves.

Carla watched her aunt out in the garden. She could see that she was talking and crying. "I'm so sorry," Carla whispered. "I didn't know it would be this bad for you."

Bonnie appeared at her shoulder. "She's takin' it real hard."

Carla nodded, but didn't reply. It irritated her that Bonnie came into the room without being invited. *I'm beginning to sound like Auntie Em,* she smiled at the thought. *I find Bonnie tiresome!* Carla almost giggled out loud. Instead, she coughed and turned away.

"You okay?" Bonnie asked.

"Yes, I'm fine," Carla responded. "Don't you have work to do or something?" She tried to sound stern, but it came out lame to her own ears.

"Yes, I do," Bonnie answered. "You know I care about you all," she added.

"You're not family," Carla suddenly felt angry. "You are hired help who happens to live here. Please, go back to work." Carla didn't turn from the window as Bonnie left the room. She heard her singing somewhere in the house. It irritated her more that Bonnie seemed content to work and didn't argue. *I don't want to be like Auntie Em, but I can see how she feels about some people that seem to be here too long. She must not feel close to almost anybody, so why me? What is our connection?* She noticed Mary Maude was walking toward the barn. "I wonder what she's doing?" Carla muttered, sounding every bit like her aunt.

Carla saw Lester come out of the barn and he and Mary Maude talked for a few moments. *What do they have to talk about?* Came the unbidden thought. *Why should I care? Why do I feel irritated about it?* "Wow!" She said aloud. "I am freakin' paranoid!" She turned from the window and marched down the stairs. She couldn't help noticing Phillip standing in the loft of the barn, also watching the conversation below. "Is this what she's done her whole life?" Carla mused as she walked along the hallway. She stood for a moment looking down from the landing to the hallway below her. *If someone fell from right here, they could land in front of that old closet and maybe some blood would seep onto the floor, under that carpet. Maybe what I read isn't sinister, but really is accidents and runaways. Maybe I should throw away that old diary so I'm not always searching for something wrong. But, what about Mama? She was sure Auntie Em pushed her and that her own mother might have helped or tried to dump her out of the chair so it would fall on top of her. What if grandma was just trying to stop the chair from going down the stairs? What if they both were? What if Mama was just too close to the stairs in her wheelchair and both grandma and Auntie Em were trying to save her? What if Ellie was wrong and Donna Sue really did run away? What if, what if, what if?* Carla shook her head. "I don't know and I don't want to think about it anymore. I want to live a normal life without thinking about stuff that just keeps me worried and looking for shadows or ghosts all the time." A sigh filled the hallway like a hiss.

The B&B began to pick up reservations almost every weekend and a few during the week. Most were one night only, perhaps two. Mary Maude began to fit into the routine better, but when she didn't, she reacted strongly, almost violently. She would yell at people, and not just the people who lived with her. She got angry with guests, too.

"You're driving away the guests," Carla complained to her.

"Good!" She yelled back.

"How do you expect this business to succeed? We've put a lot of effort into it, you know."

"I don't," Mary Maude retorted hotly. "And...and you are the one expecting it to be a success, whatever that means. Get away from me! Don't talk to me!"

"Auntie Em," Carla began to try reasoning.

"I said to get away from me," Mary Maude snarled. "I don't want to talk about it. I just want to be alone." She threw up her arms. "I really just want all of you to be gone. Why don't you get out? I don't want you here." With that, Mary Maude sped away, walking swiftly toward the boardwalk.

Carla watched her go. It would do no good to chase after her or to insist that she talk. It was over, done. "I can't just cancel all these reservations, any more than I can cancel the Holidays," she said quietly. "What does she expect me to do? I know she doesn't want me to leave. She's just acting out. It's a habit she started when she was a child. And her Papa isn't here to fix it." She lost sight of her aunt as she walked around the pond. "And Mister Sam left her, too."

"She don't mean it, you know," Bonnie said from the doorway of the house.

"I know that!" Carla snapped.

"Just tryin' to help. Sorry if I stepped on toes."

"Go back to work, Bonnie. I don't need your advice. I know you want to help, but it's tir... annoying." *I almost said tiresome,* Carla realized. *Geez, I am turning into her. I wonder why I don't take after my Mama?* She shook her head before going into the house to see what cleaning needed to be finished.

Later, Mary Maude wanted to play Canasta. Carla didn't feel like playing, but agreed in the interest of allowing her aunt to apologize by interacting, not really saying that she was sorry, or anything like it. Lester and Bonnie joined and they did have fun. Finally, it was bedtime. Carla yawned big.

"I'll do the dishes so you can go on to bed. You look real tired," Bonnie said.

"There gonna be a bunch of people here this weekend?" Mary Maude asked.

Carla shook her head. "Only two."

"How long?"

"Just one night."

"Well, I guess that's all right, then." Mary Maude smiled weakly.

Carla reached out and patted Mary Maude's hand. Mary Maude grabbed ahold of Carla's hand and held on tight. "I didn't know it would be so bad. I mean I just think about strangers being here and I get all stove up inside, you know? I can't breathe and can't stop my heart from poundin' like it's gonna come right out through my chest."

"I didn't know it gave you a panic attack." Carla said. "Perhaps we really should close it down after the holidays."

"No!" Mary Maude griped Carla's hand tighter.

Carla tried to pull away. "Auntie Em, you're hurting me."

She let go immediately. "I'm sorry," she said quietly. "I just don't know what to do, but I want you to be a success in this. It will keep the old house in the family. One day I hate it and the next I can see the good in it. I'm just a crazy old woman."

"But how can we keep you from feeling this panic?" Carla asked sincerely.

"It's what always happens," Mary Maude said quietly. "I even feel like Bonnie has been here too long." She shook her head. "I talked to Lester about it and he said he'd try to keep her from bothering me, but just knowin' she's here sets my teeth on edge, if you know what I mean."

Carla gave a sly smile. "I find myself irritated with her, too," she said.

"She's tiresome ain't she?" Mary Maude said, looking with more interest at her niece.

"No!" Carla said quickly. "I mean, well," she remembered thinking that very word in relation to Bonnie, herself. "Well, I suppose, but if Lester is going to keep her out of the way, it will help."

Mary Maude sighed. "Mama would take care of it," she muttered.

Carla changed the subject. "I'm thinkin' about hirin' some day labor for the house. That way, Bonnie can stay outside with Lester and not be underfoot in here. What do you think about that?"

Mary Maude slumped on the table. "More strangers? What you thinkin' girl?"

"Well just day labor. Someone to be here to clean up the used rooms and then go home. They won't stay and won't be eating with us or anything like that. You'll barely even see her."

"So, just like a hotel maid?"

"Yeah, and you won't even have to interact with her, either."

"Well…." Mary Maude started.

"I promise, Auntie Em. One girl, in and out in an hour or so, and then gone until we need her another morning." She paused to see how her aunt was receiving the news. "It will keep Bonnie outside and at her own house, so we won't have to deal with her at all most of the time.

"Well, ain't that just a fine howdy-do," said Bonnie. She had come into the room from the kitchen without them noticing. "I've only ever tried to help out here and this is how I get treated?"

"Believe me, Bonnie," Carla said dryly. "It's better this way. You don't want to overstay your welcome in this house."

Mary Maude stared at Carla, not knowing what to say.

"I thought we was friends, almost family. Is this how you treat family? No wonder you don't have no one."

"Bonnie, you just shut up, now," Mary Maude said with rising anger.

"Well, what do you expect?" Bonnie was close to tears.

Carla got up and went to the back door. "Lester! Lester!" She called. "You need to come up to the house!"

Lester dropped the hoe he was using and ran for the house. He was out of breath. "What's happened?" He asked.

Carla shook her head. "No, you just need to take Bonnie out of the house. She's irritating Mary Maude and you need to get her away. You know what can happen."

"Yes, Ma'am," he nodded. Without waiting any longer, he headed into the house.

*　*　*　*　*

The business went on as planned. It seemed that during the holidays, Mary Maude enjoyed the excitement of decorating and making her nearly famous goodies. She avoided the strangers as much as possible, and Bonnie, too. She didn't mind cooking, but didn't want to serve the food, so Carla hired a girl who did that work. Mary Maude didn't complain about the extra help, but Carla made sure the girls that she hired came and went quietly. They had very little contact with anyone other than Carla, except when they had to serve food. Mary Maude scared the three girls who were sent to them by the temporary employment agency.

At the end of the holidays, just after New Year's, Mary Maude asked to see the accounts for the business. Carla duly produced ledger pages she knew her aunt would expect, hand-written and old-fashioned, but developed from a spreadsheet Carla used on the computer.

"Why are you hiring people from some agency?" Mary Maude asked. "We always just got girls off the street. They worked out fine for us. Have we gone all fancy or something?"

"No-o-o," Carla drawled. "It's just simple to call them up and they send the help we need."

"You're paying them too much," she complained.

"It's the going wage for the work they do."

"Why are there three of them? I thought you were just hiring one girl. I haven't seen three of them. Are they gypin' us?"

"No, Auntie. They send which ever girl is available when we need someone. It isn't always the same girl. But I do try to have only one of them help with the breakfast, if possible."

"They only work five hours a day?" Mary Maude looked incredulous.

"Yes, just a few hours on the days we have guests. That's all we need."

"Well, I don't like it."

"Would you rather do all the work yourself?" Carla's voice was testy and she looked accusingly at her aunt.

"Who do you think you are?" Mary Maude stared at her niece. "This is my home. Sam and I own it and we make the rules here."

143

"And I also live here."

"But, you don't own it. We do. Go ask Mister Sam yourself. He'll set you straight about who owns what."

Carla looked perplexed, turning her head to one side. "How am I gonna ask Sam?"

"Why, just walk out to the barn. He's bound to be workin' there or in the orchard…" her voice trailed off as she looked out the window toward the barn.

Carla's voice became softer. "Are you okay, Auntie Em?"

"Don't talk to me!" She snapped. Without another word, Mary Maude walked outside. Carla watched her walk around the garden, ending in front of the family graves. She dropped to her knees and hid her face in her hands.

Carla sighed, turning away from the window. She gathered up the accounting papers and placed them neatly on the desk, got out the dust mop and began cleaning the house. It helped her to stay grounded, like life was some kind of normal.

Later, she had to listen to Bonnie complain about how Lester was making her go for boat rides or walks around "that stupid lake or pond, or whatever it is. Ugly water hole, I say. Scares me to death and he knows it, too. But, he takes me out there anyways. I'm gonna die out there, you know."

"You're exaggerating, Bonnie. He's just trying to distract you from annoying Auntie Em."

"Well, I suppose." Bonnie said quietly. "Still, I get awful scared, especially in one of those little rowboats."

"Maybe you should learn to swim…" Carla began.

"At my age?" Bonnie barked out a dry laugh. "I'm not gettin' in water with fish and frogs and snakes and bugs, ewwww!"

Carla laughed. "Okay, okay, I get it."

Bonnie started to walk out, going to her own apartment. She turned at the door. "Am I really that annoying?" She asked, tears threatening.

"You know how intolerant my aunt is of most people, Bonnie." Carla explained.

"Yes, but you said..." Bonnie stopped, evidently too choked up to continue. "I didn't think you would be so much like her." With that, Bonnie walked out.

Am I? Carla thought. *Am I so much like Auntie Em? She remembered her own words about Bonnie, how she felt the woman was becoming tiresome. But, I'm not making people disappear like she did when she was my age, and younger. I'm fixing that problem, aren't I? That makes me decidedly unlike her.* A huge sigh escaped her as she turned to climb the stairs to her bedroom. It was still fairly early, but she suddenly felt exhausted.

CHAPTER ELEVEN

Reservations kept coming and Carla accepted them over the winter and into spring. Mary Maude did the cooking and kept the kitchen spotless. She also took care of the laundry. She allowed Carla to buy an automatic washer and dryer. She had to admit that the clothes were softer and smelled good. However, once in a while, she hung out the wash because she loved the smell of fresh air in her towels.

Bonnie continued to help clean the house along with her outside chores she and Lester did. Phillip died, evidently of natural causes, one night as the spring peepers were singing in the moonlight around the pond. Lester reported the death to Mary Maude and cremated the body the next day. There were no guests, so the light spiral of smoke didn't bother anyone. He spread the ashes over the roses as was the custom of the house. Bonnie complained to her husband, but didn't offer to call 9-1-1 or insist on a "proper burial."

Carla found Mary Maude sitting on the patio and brought her a cup of tea. Mary Maude smiled up at her. "Sit with me a spell," she offered.

Carla sat. "It's nice weather again finally," she observed.

"Yep," Mary Maude said. "I'm gettin' old, Carla."

"Not that old, yet, Auntie." Carla protested.

"I'm not gonna argue with you, but I feel old." A sigh escaped her.

"That's good. I don't want to argue, either." Carla nodded.

"I always hoped I'd have me a daughter, but I guess you'll have to do," she said with a straight face.

"Thanks," Carla answered in the same tone.

Mary Maude laughed aloud. It was the first time that laugh had been heard at the house for a very long time. Carla couldn't help but laugh with her.

"I miss Mister Sam," Mary Maude said suddenly.

"Yeah," Carla agreed.

"No, I mean, he always knew what I needed. Papa taught him well and he never let me down. Now, I just get frustrated because I don't have anyone to bully. I need that. You bring lots of strangers here, but it isn't the same. I can't … it just doesn't work anymore. I'm sad and angry all the time." She paused. "Oh, hell, I can't explain it. Ain't nobody who understands." She looked thoughtfully at the barn. "Lester comes closest. He knows, but he never had to do nothin' but what Sam said. It just ain't the same."

Carla didn't know what to say, so she kept quiet.

"Don't you be afraid of me, Girl. I don't look on you the same as the street girls who used to come here."

"I'm not afraid, but I am sad. What can I do?"

"Can you get me a live-in maid just this once?"

"No. I won't do that, Auntie Em. I'm not going to be a part of that." Carla shook her head slowly, but with determination.

Mary Maude stood suddenly and walked away.

"I'm going to town for groceries!" Carla called after her. "Do you want anything that isn't on the list?"

Mary Maude waved her away and kept walking, past the barn and out toward the field.

Carla left for her shopping trip to replenish the food supplies they had used up. When Carla walked out of the grocery store, a young woman was standing beside her car. "What are you doing?" Carla asked with a frown.

'Oh, hi, um, I was wondering if you need some help," the girl said nervously.

I'm pretty sure I can handle these groceries," Carla said as she opened the trunk.

The girl laughed. "No, I mean, um, could you use some help out to your house, you know?"

"Why would you think I need help at my house?" Carla felt trapped, like Mary Maude must have set this up.

"Oh. Well, you own the B&B, right?" She didn't wait for an answer. "I know a couple of people who have worked out there for you, so I was just wondering if you might hire me."

Carla sighed as she continued to put groceries in the trunk. "So you want to be on my day-labor list?" Carla gave a half-smile. "You'd have to contact the employment agency downtown."

"Day labor?" The girl shook her head. "No-o-o, I was thinkin' more of a real job, you know. Like, I mean some real cleanin' and cookin' and stuff like that."

Carla shut the trunk with a bang. "Where do you live?" She asked with irritation in her shaking voice.

"Um, a-across town," the girl stammered.

"With your family?"

"No," the girl looked down at her tattered jeans and worn out shoes.

Carla closed her eyes and tried to remain breathing evenly. *Don't do it, said her inner voice. Don't take this girl out there.*

"I'll work real hard," the girl pleaded. "I promise I will. I'm good at cleanin' and stuff. I can cook real good, too. I know how to make bread and rolls. I can help out and make a real difference, if you'll just give me a chance."

"Do you have a way to get out there everyday?"

"Huh?" She cocked her head to one side

"Do you have a ride to come to work and get home again?" Carla said slowly, dreading the answer.

"Well, I was kinda hopin' you would let me stay out there," the girl said.

No! Carla was screaming inside. "What's your name?"

"Diana. Sorry, I should'a introduced myself."

"It's okay. I'm Carla."

"Do you own that old farm?"

"No, it belongs to my aunt."

"The old witch-lady?"

"What?" Carla couldn't help smiling.

Diana blushed. "I, I'm sorry. That's just what some people say about the old woman out there."

"Really?" Carla asked. "I never heard that before."

"I shouldn't have said nothing," Diana was scraping her toe along the pavement.

Carla smiled. "It's all right. She can be strange sometimes. I guess people could think she acts like a witch."

"So, will ya hire me?" Diana asked, looking hopeful.

"How old are you?"

"Twenty," she said quickly.

"Eighteen?" Carla asked.

"No, I really am twenty," Diana smiled. She reached into a pocket and produced a driver's license.

"This says you live down in Franklin," Carla looked askance at Diana.

"Yeah, well, I haven't been there for awhile. My daddy's in prison and I'm not sure where Ma is, exactly. My step-dad is not somebody I wanted to stay around without Ma there, you get the drift?"

Carla nodded. "Yeah," she said with resignation. "Get in. I'll do what I can for you."

Diana beamed. "Oh, thank you!" She gushed. "You won't be sorry, I promise."

I'm already sorry, Carla thought. *I will have to keep an eye on you, and you just don't know what can happen. It better not, but, oh, I don't even want to think anymore.*

Mary Maude couldn't believe that Carla brought Diana to the house. "Where'd you find her?" She asked. The excitement in her voice and her eyes almost made Carla sick.

"She found me," Carla said as she was trying to put groceries away.

"God's good, ain't that so?" Mary Maude asked.

"God?" Carla asked in confusion. "What's He got to do with it?"

"Why, this is an answer to my prayers, don't cha know?" Mary Maude smiled broadly. "I'll take real good care of this one, I promise. You'll see. It will be all right."

"Until it isn't," Carla muttered as she walked up the stairs to her room.

"What's that?" Mary Maude called after her.

"I'm gonna change and show Diana what to do. Is that all right/'

Mary Maude pouted. "I want to, Carla. I'm just so excited to have someone here to share our home with."

"Fine. I'm going to change and go for a walk, then." She disappeared into her room.

Diana worked out well. She was knowledgeable about foods and pleased Mary Maude by baking beautiful desserts and fancy meals for guests and for the family. She was good at cleaning up, too. She cleaned in other rooms when she wasn't busy in the kitchen, but Mary Maude kept her cooking and baking and canning foods, too.

Carla concerned herself with the business and her own chores. She was the one who did the shopping like Sam used to do. She and Lester went to the mill for feed for the animals or to make arrangements to have feed and hay delivered. Lester still did the butchering and gathered the eggs. Bonnie helped with the lawn and gardens, her natural ability to landscape making the old place beautiful. Carla often went for walks around the pond. Lester had a couple of benches installed and she loved to sit and watch the ducks that gathered on the water. Also, she often saw fish jump and swim near the boardwalk and pier. She rarely took out a boat, but she knew that Lester often did so he could catch some fish and jig frogs. It was a welcome addition to their diet. Life seemed to take on a natural routine and a form of normalcy. But, Carla wasn't fooled. She knew it couldn't last because Mary Maude couldn't be settled for long. Also, Carla was more and more irritated by Bonnie. She couldn't figure out why she was irritated, but the truth of it was, that it was so. She sighed and threw a stick into the pond before walking back to the house to welcome some weekend guests.

Mary Maude was in a rare mood. She was humming while she cleaned up in the kitchen, ordering Diana around like a harried maid. Diana didn't seem to mind. She followed orders well and was polite to everyone. Carla watched them for a few moments before she went into the dining room and then on to the sitting room where she heard voices. There was a lot of talk about local antique shops and other attractions. Finally, everyone headed up to bed. Carla looked around, making sure the house was clean and that nothing had been left undone. She paused by the large, oak table, running a hand lightly over the polished wood. The table was set perfectly for tomorrow's breakfast. Somehow, it made her sad but she wasn't sure why.

"That Diana's a real good worker," Bonnie said softly from the kitchen doorway. "She's got everything set up to make breakfast already."

Carla looked up. "Yeah, I was noticing that."

"I reckon she's gonna work out real well. Miz Maude seems to like her just fine."

"For now," Carla said softly. "They always please her at first, you know."

Bonnie nodded. "True. But they don't all work this hard and try to be so pleasing."

"You did," Carla pointed out.

"Yeah, and I'm older. These young girls usually don't want to work or only do half jobs. Diana goes out of her way to do everything right down to the line."

"You girls gossipin' about me?" Mary Maude asked sharply, coming through the kitchen.

"Why, no Ma'am," Bonnie blustered. "We was just sayin' how good the house looks."

"Hmph," Mary Maude spluttered. "I heard my name. I know youse was talkin' 'bout me."

"Well, I did say that I thought you was happy with the new girl," Bonnie said.

"Good night," Carla said as she turned to the stairs running up them two at a time. She flopped across her bed, looking up at the ceiling. "Arrrrrrrgh," she said in frustration.

"You sassin' me, Girl?" Mary Maude's voice came from the doorway.

"I shut my door for a reason, Auntie Em," she complained with a sigh.

"And I opened it."

"Well, close it again when you go to bed, please."

"You mad at me?" Mary Maude asked.

Carla sat up to look at her aunt. "No, I'm not mad. I'm worried, but I'm not mad."

"P-shaw!" Mary Maude exclaimed. "You don't have nothin' to be worried about. Diana is a good helper and I want to keep her here forever, just like you." Mary Maude smiled broadly, showing her rotting teeth. "You ain't jealous, are you?"

Carla shook her head, closing her eyes and rubbing her forehead. "No, I just know when you get tired of her, I will need to step in and take her away. That's just how it will have to be."

Mary Maude came over and sat next to Carla on the bed. She twisted the hem of her apron. "All right, Carla. That sounds just fine. That's what Papa used to do, you know? When I was a little girl and Mama and I needed to have someone new. You can do that."

Carla sighed. "Do you mean it?"

"'Course I do. But, if it doesn't work out, well…"

"No!" Carla said hotly. "There won't be any not working out. We have a plan and we will stick to it. No more sugar shack. Is that understood?"

Mary Maude stood up, looking closely at her niece. She turned to the door, but lingered there, running her fingers along the door jamb. "You don't get to tell me, Carla. I know who I am and I made peace with me a long time ago. Sam understood me and he too, did what he did to preserve who I am." She nodded her head toward the window across the room. "Lester knows, but his understanding is not the same. Not yet. He will come into it, though, just wait and see."

"Stop, Auntie Em," Carla pleaded. "Please stop talking like this is all normal."

Mary Maude laughed with no humor, a dry, raspy sound. "You are more like me than you want to admit. Don't think you aren't. I know you, too."

"Get out of my room," Carla growled, tears running down her cheeks. "I don't want you here."

"Am I getting tiresome?" Mary Maude asked sarcastically.

"Don't!" Carla hissed, rising from the bed.

"Or what?"

"I don't know!" Carla threw her hands up into the air. "Get away from me!"

Mary Maude fixed Carla with a pointed, yet somehow evil, smile. "You are yelling, Carla. There are guests in the house, and it is rude. I am going to my room now to let you calm down, but don't you ever threaten me again. Did you hear me?"

"Yes," Carla breathed between clenched teeth. Her arms were at her sides, fists clenched. She couldn't wait for her aunt to leave the room. She didn't look up, but she did hear the door close. She sat back down as she tried to breathe slowly and deeply. Finally, she laid back on the bed and cried herself to sleep.

There was noise, talking. Carla couldn't make out what was being said, it all seemed confused and distant. She opened her eyes, realizing she was still in bed and the guests were up and about. She heard someone on the stairs. "Oh, don't fall!" Someone called. "These stairs are kind of steep. It's a good thing you have those treads on there." Carla couldn't hear anymore as the guests made their way to the dining room. She could smell the faint odor of bacon and maybe coffee. She breathed deeply and was rewarded with the spicy smell of cinnamon. "Diana must have been baking again," she smiled. When she sat up, she was reminded of the argument she'd had with her aunt the night before. "Ahhhh," I need to apologize," she murmured as she reached for her clothes.

Carla greeted the guests and sat with them for a little while. They were leaving this morning and talked about their plans for the day. Carla bid them farewell, excusing herself to go to the kitchen where Mary Maude was standing at the sink, washing dishes as usual. Carla came up behind her and put her arms around her waist, tightly. "I love you," she whispered. "I'm sorry we argued. I don't want that to happen again."

Mary Maude didn't respond. She just kept washing a greasy pan.

Carla stepped back, waiting. Nothing happened, however. Carla sighed and fixed herself a cup of peppermint tea. She fixed one for her aunt, too and left it on the counter. "I'm going for a walk," she said as she carried her cup out the backdoor. It was cold so she didn't stay outside long. When she returned to the kitchen, Mary Maude was not there, but she had taken the tea, so Carla felt a little better. She washed out her cup and began cleaning in the living room. She heard the sound of the washer in the basement which answered the question about where her aunt was. Bonnie was washing windows and Carla could hear Diana in the bedrooms upstairs. Carla stepped to the desk to check her calendar. No more guests for a week. That would give a few days for them all to relax, to not get in each other's way. It was a long day, time passing slowly even though everyone was busy. The problem was that no one was talking. Everyone was walking on eggshells around both Mary Maude and Carla. Even Lester just came in for meals and left again. Carla wondered how long her aunt would keep this going, keep everyone at arm's length from one another. She failed to see that she was very much like her aunt and was part of the silence herself.

Two days. Two days of practical silence. Two days of thinking and thinking again. Carla was ready to give in. She decided to be bubbly at breakfast and suggested a picnic for lunch. The weather was fine with not a cloud in the sky. She quickly took a shower and went to the kitchen.

To her surprise, she found Mary Maude humming at the stove. "Good morning, Auntie Em," Carla said brightly.

Mary Maude turned and smiled at her. "Good morning Dear. I'm making peanut butter pancakes."

Carla frowned. "Ewww," she said.

Mary Maude laughed out loud. "That was a joke," she announced. "It's just blueberry pancakes and scrambled eggs."

Breakfast went well with everyone more animated. They made plans for the picnic down by the lake. That appealed to everyone but Bonnie, of course, but she said she'd just stay away from the water. However, Lester insisted that she go for a boat ride and everyone urged her on.

They walked toward the pier to watch as Lester literally lifted Bonnie and plopped her into one of the rowboats. The boat rocked back and forth until Lester got in and held fast to the pier to settle the boat and the water as well. "You're all gonna be the death of me!" She yelled from the boat as Lester rowed to the center of the lake.

Carla choked on her food and Mary Maude slapped her on the back, laughing so hard she began to choke as well. Diana stared at them both, unsure what the joke was about.

"I'm with Bonnie," Diana said when everyone had calmed down. She shuddered. "I don't like water, either."

"Why?" Carla managed to ask.

"I bout drowned when I was a little girl," she said sadly. "My Ma tried to drown me in the tub."

"Whatever for?" Mary Maude asked with interest.

"I don't know. I was really little, like two or three. I think I was just in the way."

"But, she still raised you, right?" Carla asked.

"Yeah, well she was there, but she and Paul, that was her husband, they did Meth and stuff, were drunk or high a lot. Then she just went away." Diana got a faraway look in her eyes. "Paul said she just run off, but I always thought he killed her. Buried her in the back yard or the basement, or somewhere, I don't know." She suddenly looked around at them and out toward the boat. "Anyway, I ran off, too and here I am." She gave a weak smile.

Mary Maude had tears in her eyes which surprised Carla. "You can stay here and be my daughter," she said, patting Diana's hand.

"I'd like that," she said softly. "But, I don't want to take Carla's place."

Mary Maude said, "I never had a baby that lived. I should have, but, well that just didn't happen. The boys are buried right out there with

Sam and Mama and Papa. So, you be my daughter along with Carla. I adopted her."

"I'm really her niece," Carla smiled. "But, she has been like a Mama to me for quite a while now."

"I kinda thought that, but I didn't know for sure." Diana looked toward the lake again. "What is Bonnie saying? She just keeps talking and talking."

Mary Maude laughed. "That's what she does best. Yak, yak, yak."

They all laughed at that for a moment, then hand in hand, they walked back to their picnic spot. Carla began cleaning up the food, putting everything into their wicker basket. Diana and Mary Maude walked into the woods toward the sugar shack. Carla wondered what story her aunt would tell about the old building, but since it was fenced off, it wouldn't matter much. She wouldn't have to show Diana anything that would raise questions. Carla looked out at the lake once more, but couldn't see the rowboat. *They're probably beyond sight behind those reeds*, she thought.

They all heard the splash and the muffled call for help. Still, Carla couldn't see the boat. She watched in what seemed like slow motion as her aunt and Diana turned toward the lake. Diana pointed and said something, but Carla realized that she couldn't hear anything because of an odd roaring in her ears. She looked back at the lake, but the world seemed to stand still and she felt she couldn't breathe. Finally, the boat came into view, Lester rowing as hard as he could. Bonnie wasn't anywhere to be seen. He tied the boat up and began tugging on the anchor rope. Carla felt bile rise up in her throat as Lester pulled Bonnie's lifeless body from the water. He laid her onto the pier and tried to use CPR, but after a short time, looked up at Mary Maude and shook his head. Carla felt numb as she helplessly watched her aunt console the crying Diana. Lester walked toward the barn to fetch the wheelbarrow. Mary Maude and Lester talked briefly, then Carla fled to the house. She ran to the nearest bathroom where she vomited over and over. She sat weakly on the floor, hanging over the toilet, too exhausted to move. Mary Maude found her still there after she had put Diana to bed in her grief. "Come now," Mary Maude said softly. "Let's go upstairs where you can rest."

Carla allowed her aunt to take her upstairs. "What on earth happened?" She asked plaintively.

"She fell in and Lester can't swim so he couldn't save her. That's all there is to it, a tragic accident." Mary Maude wagged her head sadly. "Don't make too much of it, Honey-Girl."

"Another accident?" Carla sighed. "Have you and Lester been plotting this?"

Mary Maude slapped a hand to her chest. "Good Heavens, no!" She exclaimed. "What you think I am?"

"I'm just...I just can't believe it. We were all right there, but he rowed that boat out of our sight."

"You have the biggest imagination, Carla. He was rowing around the lake like he always does. Now that there's been an accident, you want to make it out to be something else."

"What are we gonna do?"

"'Bout what?"

"Has he already taken her to the sugar shack?"

Mary Maude nodded. "Yes, Child. Let's not talk about it anymore, okay?" She pushed Carla down on the bed and tucked a blanket around her. "Sleep and don't worry. Soon it won't matter, you know?"

Carla did sleep, though she didn't intend to. She got up sometime around midnight to take a hot shower, then went to the kitchen for some tea. She could see a light on out in the sugar shack and wondered idly what Lester could be doing out there. She imagined him shoving Bonnie's body into the furnace and shuddered at the thought. "One more," she breathed. "One more," she put her head back, trying to breathe deeply, with her eyes closed. She was roused from her position by the tea kettle whistling.

"Midnight tea, how fine," Mary Maude said as she turned off the kettle and got out cups for them both.

Carla wasn't surprised that her aunt had appeared in the kitchen. *She moves around here like a ghost,* Carla thought. *Maybe she is a ghost. Maybe this is all a dream or I've gone mad. Maybe none of this has been real at all.* She felt detached, like she was watching life from far away. *Is this what it's like to go insane?* She pondered.

Mary Maude led Carla to the table where she poured four cups of tea. Soon, Diana joined them and Lester walked in from outside. "We're all sad," Mary Maude said. "But, what is done is done." She looked pointedly at Lester, who hung his head without speaking. "Don't let's make more of it than it is."

Silence filled the room for several minutes. "Are there guests comin' soon?" Mary Maude asked.

Carla looked up as if she had been punched. "Guests?" She asked. "I, I don't know Auntie Em." She tried to swallow some tea. "I'll have to look at the calendar."

"I already did," Mary Maude smiled. "And there are two coming on Saturday for the fishing derby on the river."

"I'll make sure the rooms are cleaned," Diana offered.

"Good," Mary Maude nodded. "Carla, what else do we need to do?"

"Um, just take their money when they get here, if they haven't paid already," she mumbled.

"Darn it, Girl!" Mary Maude slapped the table making them all jump. "Just snap out of this and get your head together! We got a business to run and you are supposed to be on top of the paperwork and stuff! Diana and I will take care of the house, and Lester has the outside, ain't that right, Lester?"

"Yes, Ma'am," he nodded.

"There, see?" Mary Maude beamed like she had just won a prize.

Carla looked around at them all and shook herself. "I just need some more sleep." She got up to leave the room. "Is there going to be anything to do out in the garden?"

"No, Ma'am," Lester answered. "Just gonna fertilize some of the roses, you know."

Carla nodded before she fled to her bedroom. She closed the door and put her chair against it. "How can she do this?" Carla mumbled. "I mean, I know I didn't always like Bonnie, but I didn't want this to happen to her." She looked out the window. There was still smoke coming from the woods. A thin tendril of white smoke like always. "Was it an accident?" Carla closed her eyes while she felt her way to the bed. She laid down, but had no intention of sleeping. She hugged her knees and sobbed into her folded arms. "Oh, Mama! I need you so much!" After a time, Carla laid on her quilt and drifted into an uneasy sleep, one filled with dreams of girls walking in a fog, pointing at Carla and laughing. "I wonder what he does with them?" They mocked. When she awoke, she was drenched with sweat and tears. She could barely remember the dreams, but just enough to feel drained and afraid.

CHAPTER TWELVE

Somehow, they all carried on like life was normal. Carla booked guests, Diana did almost all the cleaning single-handedly, and Mary Maude cooked and kept herself busy in the kitchen. Lester did a good job outside, seeming to know about the shrubs Bonnie had planted and he kept the yard looking nice. From the street, the home was inviting. The little lake was a favorite for guests who took advantage of boat rides and fishing. Some simply enjoyed the boardwalk and eating breakfast on the patio in the fine, summer weather. Everyone remarked about the beauty of the rose garden. Lester smiled in pride.

They played games in the evening, Mary Maude's favorite being Euchre. There was a lot of laughter and Carla settled into the life with little thought about her "spring breakdown" as she thought of it.

As summer wore on, both Mary Maude and Carla became argumentative, mostly with one another. Mary Maude was becoming irritated with the number of guests that they were serving, and Carla wanted to pack the house with more and more people. "You just want to drive me crazy so you can take over!" Mary Maude accused, standing in the doorway of the dining room.

"You are crazy," Carla mumbled, regretting it immediately. "No! I didn't mean it," she said as Mary Maude turned menacingly toward her.

"What did you say?" Mary Maude growled.

"I, I'm sorry. I didn't mean to say that," Carla pleaded.

"You didn't mean to say it out loud, you mean," Mary Maude continued, her face contorting in her anger.

"No, no, no, no," Carla wagged her head, putting her hands up on both sides of her head. "We've been so busy, and I'm tired. I just snapped out something hurtful and I'm sorry. Please, Auntie Em, I really am."

"I don't know how to believe you," Mary Maude said with more control. "I've never let anybody talk to me the way you do. I've given you everything and you treat me like, well, like I don't even know what." She paused. "Is this how a girl treats her mother?"

You're not my mother, Carla thought with her eyes closed. "No, of course not," she choked out.

"How many more people are gonna come through here before we get a break from all that?" Mary Maude asked. Her voice still had a hint of her anger.

"Every week until Labor Day," Carla said. "Then, one or two weekends in October."

"So, we don't get any summer at all, you're sayin'."

"Well, no, I guess not." Carla was thoughtful. "Did you want to have a vacation or something?"

"Don't be smart with me!" Mary Maude snapped back.

Carla sighed. "Again, forgive me," she said as she got up from the desk and closed the laptop computer. "I'm going for a walk. Maybe we can start over and not argue."

Mary Maude didn't respond, just watched as her niece walked out the door.

"What do you need done, Miz Maude," asked Diana sweetly.

"Shaddup, Girl!" Mary Maude barked. "You know what to do. Don't go trying to please me. That gets tiresome real quick.

Diana disappeared to find some cleaning she could do.

The next two weeks went by slowly as Carla and Mary Maude tried to be civil with each other. Diana kept going first to one of them and then the other, offering her help and trying to talk about "what might be wrong."

"Stop it, Diana!" Carla told her one day. "You are getting so tiresome and I don't need you sneaking around between Auntie Em and me."

"That's what Miz Maude told me," Diana said with a dejected look.

"What?"

"That I'm tiresome," she replied.

"When did she say that?" Carla asked with concern.

"I don't know, a couple of weeks ago, I guess."

"Maybe it's time for you to move on," Carla said in a half-whisper.

"You firin' me?" Diana asked.

"No, my aunt wouldn't be pleased about that," Carla said. "Listen, Diana. You have to do your work without complaining and stay out of the way. Keep us stocked with your wonderful desserts and maybe you'll be all right." Carla paused. "Promise me!" She said with urgency in her voice.

"Okay," Diana said, unsure of what was happening. "I don't do much complaining, so I'll just do my job and not bug the two of you."

"Good. Good," Carla said with a quick smile, a smile that didn't quite make it to her eyes.

$$* \quad * \quad * \quad * \quad *$$

One weekend, Lester got some company. He introduced them to Carla and Mary Maude. "This here is Jeffrey," he said of the younger man. "He helped me with my apartment out there over the garage." Lester smiled as though he had found a treasure. "And this is Jerome," he turned to the older man. "He's Jeff's father."

"Hm," answered Mary Maude.

"They, uh, want a job, Miz Maude," Lester half apologized.

"Doin' what?" Mary Maude asked with a huge frown.

"I've worked many years as a butler, Ma'am," Jerome said with a slight smile. "And my son here," he pointed at Jeff. "He's a good carpenter."

"What do we need with a butler and a carpenter?" Mary Maude asked.

Lester looked down at the floor and sighed." I just thought it might be good to have some help with the farm work and the yard and garden." He looked at Mary Maude then back down again. "Then I thought that maybe a butler would work out better than maids have," Lester said.

Carla couldn't help smiling. *Maybe this was the answer*, she thought. She looked askance at Mary Maude, raising her eyebrows.

"You can't be serious," Mary Maude said. "A man? In the house?" She shook her head in disbelief.

"Let's give it a try," Carla said, elbowing her aunt in the side. "It might be good for business to have a butler."

"I'll tell you what," Jerome added. "Jeff and I will work here for a month and you see if it works out."

"Where you think you're gonna stay?" Mary Maude demanded. "Not here with us!"

Jerome smiled. "Lester has offered for us to stay with him out over the garage," he answered.

"Well, that's settled," Carla snickered.

"I'll be...." Mary Maude began. "What kind of pay you expectin?"

"Lester said that there is some money from the farm that might be used for our upkeep. We don't have a regular home, you see."

"So, you're a homeless butler and carpenter?"

Jerome laughed. "I guess you could say that. My wife died and we lived with her family. They didn't want us there anymore."

"And you don't have jobs, either?"

He shook his head. "No, Ma'am, not right now. Jeff, here, does some day labor, but I've been out of work for some time, taking care of my wife, who was an invalid after a car wreck."

"Don't get in the way," Mary Maude said, then in an aside to Carla. "Here we go again, filling up the house with people. Good God!" With that, she went upstairs where she shut herself into her bedroom, away from everyone.

Jerome turned out to be very good at his job. He was excellent with the guests and always had tea or lemonade ready for Mary Maude. They almost never saw Jeff at all, as his work was outside on the farm.

It soon became clear that Diana and Jeff were attracted to each other. They spent every spare moment together and it came as no surprise when they announced they wanted to get married.

"This is a house of love," declared Mary Maude at breakfast one morning, awe filling her voice. "Everybody finds somebody here. I found my Sam, Lester had Bonnie, and now Diana has Jeffrey. That," she pointed at Carla. "Just leaves you."

Carla gave her aunt a disdainful look. "Right. I tried that once, remember?"

"Well, there's always Jerome," Mary Maude whispered, pointing at the retreating figure of the butler, going to the kitchen.

"He's more your age than mine," Carla whispered back.

"Sam was a fair bit older than me, you'll remember," Mary Maude said aloud.

"Sh-h-h," Carla spluttered. "He'll hear you."

"So," Mary Maude gave her a knowing wink. "You have noticed him."

"No, well I mean, of course, because he's a fine-looking man. But, no I'm not in the market for a man in my life."

"It would be almost perfect," Mary Maude went on dreamily. "Why don't you ask him to take you out somewhere?"

"Are you kidding?" Carla asked, forgetting to whisper. "I mean, no, that's not how it's done." She cocked her head to one side. "Is it?"

Mary Maude laughed loud and long.

Neither of them noticed Jerome come back into the room until he spoke. "Will that be all this morning, Ma'am?" He asked.

"Oh! Jerome you scared me half to death!" Mary Maude waved a hand at him.

"Miss Diana is out there doing up the dishes and baking something that smells delicious. I dusted the sitting room and I would like to go into town for a little bit, if that's all right."

"Sure," Mary Maude said.

"There's a list in the kitchen," Carla said at the same time.

Jerome waved a paper at her. "I got the list. I was wondering if you would like to go along and show me around the place, Miss Carla?"

Mary Maude snickered.

Carla turned red, closing her eyes so she couldn't see her aunt. "I've got things to do here," she began weakly.

"I see," Jerome said.

"No she don't!" Mary Maude declared. "She's just shy and needs more than a little push to get her out the door." She turned to her niece. "You go on, now. Make sure he gets the right stuff. You know how men are. They never know what's good, just pick up the first thing they see."

Carla looked incredulously at her aunt. "As if you ever went to town yourself. You always sent Mister Sam," Carla said.

In the end, they went together. Once the shopping was done, Carla showed Jerome what there was of the town and they had supper together at a small café. Carla was more relaxed than she remembered being in a very long time. Jerome was knowledgeable and fun. At last, they realized that it was getting late so they drove back to the house.

It became a regular thing, Carla and Jerome going out for supplies. And of course, Jeff and Diana eloped and came back man and wife. They had a happy celebration of their own, six people isolated from the rest of the world. The holiday season came and went and spring was in the air once again when Carla and Mary Maude locked horns again.

"We need a break," Mary Maude said.

"From what, life?" Carla retorted.

"From people," Mary Maude answered.

"Oh, my God, not again," Carla moaned.

"You know how I am," Mary Maude said hotly. "I can only stand this for a little while and then I need a change. Once again, I am surrounded by people who are under my feet all the time. I need to make a change."

"What do you suggest?" Carla asked with a sigh of resignation.

"I need somebody to bully, Carla. You know how I am. It can't be family and everybody here is family-like."

"So, you want me to go out and get you an orphan that you can get rid of with some kind of accident, I suppose." Carla was being sarcastic.

"Exactly!" Mary Maude said with excitement.

Carla looked narrowly at her aunt, standing in the doorway of her bedroom. "No," she said firmly. "That practice is done. There will be no more accidental deaths here. Do you understand that?"

"No I don't!" Mary Maude whirled around to face Carla. She was halfway out into the hallway. "You know what I need! Why don't you want me to be happy? Everybody else around here is happy as larks!"

"No, and that's final," Carla said. "Just go for a walk and cool off. I'm not entertaining this conversation."

Mary Maude shook a finger at Carla. "You're not my boss, you know. You don't get to tell me what to do in my own house. As long as I'm alive, this place is mine and I will have it my way! I'll go get someone on my own!" She turned around and stomped toward the railing.

"You don't know how to drive…" Carla was saying when the scream filled her ears. She ran out into the hallway where her aunt had fallen over the bannister and lay in a grotesque heap on the floor below. "No-no-no-no, no, no, no!" Carla cried as she ran down the stairs. She fell to her knees beside her aunt and gently rolled her over. There was blood oozing out of her mouth and nose. Her eyes were closed in death. "No-o-o-o-o-o!" Carla screamed.

Jerome came running into the hallway and took in the scene in a second. "I'll call for a doctor," he said reaching for the wall phone.

"No!" Carla told him. "No, just go get Lester, please."

"Carla," he said gently. "We need medical help."

"It's too late for that," Carla sobbed, rocking back and forth, holding Mary Maude in her arms. "Just get Lester. He'll know what to do."

"I'll go get him," Diana said from behind Jerome.

"Who is her doctor?" Jerome persisted.

"Shut up!" Carla spat back at him. "Get away from me!"

"Oh, Lord-a-mercy," Lester declared when he came in. "What happened here?"

"She must have thought she was closer to the stairs. She turned around and went right over the railing up there," Carla half pointed at the second floor.

"I offered to get medics out here, but Miss Carla won't have it." Jerome explained.

Lester shook his head. "That ain't how we do things," he said softly. He bent down and gently tugged on Mary Maude, but Carla held on tight. "Miss Carla, let me have her now," he said.

"Put her next to Mister Sam, will you?" She looked at Lester with tears still streaming down her face. "She has to be with Sam and her boys, with her Mama and Papa."

"What do you mean to do, just bury her somewhere?" Jerome asked with concern.

"I told you to shut up," Carla growled.

"We need to call the authorities, Lester," Jerome pleaded.

"No, sir, we don't," Lester added. "I know what to do and I'll see to it that she lays with her husband and their boys out yonder in the roses."

"Pop, let 'em be," Jeff said from the doorway. "What do you need me to help you with, Lester?" He added.

"Get me the old wheelbarrow, will ya'?" Lester answered.

"Sure," Jeff started for the door.

"No, you won't," Jerome began."

"Let me have her now," Lester said to Carla. "Sit back there on the floor and let me do what I gotta do."

Jerome reached for Carla and she turned to him, arms up at first to fight him off, then standing up so she could bury her face in his shoulder. She didn't want to watch as Lester carried her aunt outside. "I need to get away from here," she said to Jerome.

"Where do you want to go?" He asked, still holding her tightly.

"Far away," she said. "For a week or maybe two, I don't know." She looked at Diana. "Will you pack me a bag, please? I can't bear to think of going upstairs now."

"Yeah, sure," Diana answered heading for the stairs.

Jerome led Carla to the kitchen to get her a cup of tea. "You'll feel differently tomorrow," he said gently.

"Will you take me away somewhere?" She asked.

"Yes, of course. I'll have Diana cancel the guests for the weekends, for as long as you like."

"No," she shook her head. "No, I just want you to take me to a motel somewhere a couple of hours or more away. Just leave me there. I'll be fine, but I need to get away and not come back for a while. You and Diana can run the B&B. I don't care. She got up and went into the dining room to her desk. She took out the checkbook and signed a few checks. "Use these to do what needs to be done. I can't right now. I don't want to see smoke from the sugar shack. I don't want to see a hole being dug. I don't want to know. I'll order a marker for her and you and Lester can put it out there," she waved a hand in the general direction of the garden.

"Carla, rest for a day or two and see if you don't feel differently," Jerome said. "You're in shock right now and this barbaric ritual is playing with your mind. Please, sleep on it and if you still want to go in the morning, I'll take you."

Diana came into the room with a small travel bag. "Got it," she said with a sad smile.

"Thank you," Carla gave a half-smile back. "At least one of you listens to me." She turned her attention back to Jerome. "Are you taking me or not? I can drive myself, you know."

Jerome sighed. "I can take you, but I think you're making a mistake."

"I left some checks for you to use for any bills that come in," she said to Diana. "Just run the B&B like normal. I'll be back eventually. I need to run away for now."

"Yes, Ma'am," Diana curtsied.

"Come along, Jerome," Carla said, grabbing the bag and her purse. She walked to the front door and paused, looking back at the spotless house. It was then she noticed the blood stain in the hallway. "Clean that the best you can," she said, pointing at the hallway before turning around and walking out the door.

Carla stayed at a very nice motel for a month. She called the house every day to check on how things were going. She ordered them to burn down the sugar shack and plow it under the soil as if it was never there. "Plant some trees or something, but get rid of the past," she said. As she relaxed in the hot tub in her room, she sighed. "It's over. It's finally over. No more accidents and tiresome girls. Rest, Auntie Em, rest. May God be gracious on you and your tortured mind. I hope you all rest in real peace from the crazy life you carved out at that old farm. I'll try to make it a new and wonderful place, I promise."

Finally, she asked Jerome to come and get her. She was ready to go home. As they drove down the street, she noticed the new sign. AUNTIE EM'S PLACE, B&B, it read in big, bold letters. "Lester and Jeff put that up just a couple of days ago," Jerome said. "Do you like it?"

"Yes," she nodded. "I do like it."

Once in the house, Carla went upstairs. She paused at the railing and looked down. There was still a faint stain on the hardwood floor. "You left a part of you behind," she said matter of factly. Instead of going to her own room, Carla went into her aunt's room. She walked around idly, ending up at the window overlooking the gardens. She noticed that the sugar shack was still in its place. She stared at it, masked by trees and brush. Fresh tears coursed down her cheeks.

Carla turned from the window and idly walked around first one room and then another, lightly touching random furniture and fixtures. She remembered first coming to the farm, how much she missed her mother and her first horror at the deaths that occurred in the house. Gradually, she worked her way to the railing above the hallway and looked down. The flash of her aunt lying on the floor came to her mind, making her catch her breath as more tears flowed down her face. A young, blond girl came into her sight, pushing a dust mop over the hardwood floors. Carla thought for a moment that she must be seeing things. She wondered if the girl was a ghost of someone who used to work in the house. Mesmerized, Carla watched as the girl went up and down the hallway. She finally looked up and smiled. "Hello," she said softly.

"Are you real?" Carla asked.

The girl laughed. "I think so," she said. "My name is Linda. Who are you?"

"Carla," Carla answered.

The girl blushed and curtsied. "Oh, excuse me, Ma'am. I didn't know I was talking to you. I won't bother you."

"You're no bother." Carla sighed. "I just got home. Who hired you?"

"I did," Jerome said from beyond her sight. He stepped out and looked up at her. "We needed a helper."

"I see," Carla whispered. "Guard her with your life, Jerome. Don't let her have any accidents."

Jerome nodded knowingly. "Do you want some peppermint tea?"

Carla smiled and nodded. Life would go on as though nothing ever happened in this sad, old house. Carla turned around and closed the door to Mary Maude's room before going to her own bedroom. She closed the door and leaned against it, surveying the tidy room. "It will be okay," she whispered.

Jerome knocked softly on her door. Carla stepped away and turned around, opening the door. "Just set it over by the window," she instructed him.

Jerome stood silently, looking out the window for a moment before turning to face Carla. "Miss Carla," he began. "Would you marry me?"

Carla stared at him. "Did Auntie Em tell you to ask me that?"

"What?" He frowned. "Your aunt is…"

"I know she's dead, Jerome," Carla broke in.

"Yes, well, I've wanted to ask you for some time," he began again.

"Why?" She snapped.

"I care deeply about you," he answered.

"You don't even know me, Jerome," she replied. "There are many things here you don't know.."

It was Jerome's turn to break in. He held up his right hand in protest. "Actually, Miss Carla, I do know about this place. While you were away, Lester told me about your aunt and her husband, about what has happened here, and how you have been caught up in it all." He paused. When she didn't respond, he went on. "I don't care, Miss Carla. I believe I love you and I would take good care of you." He became silent.

Carla looked first at the floor and then at the window. "I wonder if this is what she felt about Sam?" Carla muttered. "An inviting peacefulness." At last, she spoke to Jerome.

"I reckon we could marry, Jerome. I can't promise you some kind of great love, but I do care for you." She smiled weakly.

Jerome smiled big enough for them both. "I'll take care of everything. Don't you worry," he answered. "I'll be back, gotta get some things in order." He raced out the door and down the stairs.

"Be careful!" Carla called, alarmed at him rushing down the stairs. She had a mental image of him lying at the bottom of the stairs, but she shook it off as she heard the front door slam. It made her smile. "It really is going to be all right," she said to her reflection in the mirror. "Life will go on much as it always has," she paused to consider what that meant. Shaking her head slowly, she muttered. "They were, after all, accidents. It's not like anyone got killed on purpose." A fleeting memory of the papers in the closet crossed her consciousness. "Young girls have such imaginations." Carefully, Carla walked to the closet and dug out the old diary written by an obscure girl named Ellie. She turned to the door and walked deliberately, but very carefully across the hall and down the stairs. It surprised her that the papers were no longer in the closet. Panicked for a moment, she searched the entire closet, becoming frantic that someone had found the hidden diary pages.

"Excuse me, Ma'am," said a soft voice from behind Carla, in the hallway.

Carla clutched the diary in her hands, looking fiercely at the girl. "What do you want?" She growled.

Linda took a step back. "I, well I wonder if you are looking for these." She held out the crumpled papers.

"Why you been snooping through my things?" She heard herself, but it reminded her of Mary Maude and she shuddered.

"I cleaned the closet a while ago," the girl paused, then rushed on. "And these here papers fell to the floor. I didn't know what to do with them so I been carryin' them in my pocked ever since."

Carla grabbed the papers from her and stuck them into the back of Ellie's diary. "Did you read them?" She peered closely at the girl, looking for a lie.

Linda nodded. "Yes, Ma'am, I did." She looked down at the floor.

"And?" Carla demanded.

"I just thought they must be from a book somebody was writin' or something," Linda shrugged.

Carla was taken aback. Could this girl really be that innocent? Clearing her throat, Carla answered. "Yes, well, they belong with this old diary." She indicated the book in her hand.

Linda looked a little shocked. "Diary?" She asked. "You mean this was something that happened to somebody? Here?" She looked around the hallway as if she anticipated ghosts coming out of the walls.

"Don't be stupid!" Carla snapped back, looking pointedly at Linda. "It was written by a tiresome girl who had too much time on her hands because she didn't do any work."

Linda took the hint. "Yes, Ma'am. I will get right back to work." She tried to smile, but it was more of a grimace.

Carla walked through the kitchen, glad that Diana was nowhere in sight. She heard the thump of the washer in the basement and guessed that Diana was busy with laundry. Carla carefully opened the back door and walked into the porch. "This is where my grandfather died," she murmured. "Will I always picture where people died now?" She shook her head to rid herself of the thoughts. Taking a huge breath, she opened the door and stepped onto the patio. She was suddenly filled with memories of days spent sitting out here with Auntie Em, Sam, Lester and Bonnie. Tears filled her eyes. She clutched the book closer to her bosom. "I'm not sure I can do this," she whispered.

Carla stood rooted to the spot for several moments before stepping with determination onto the lawn and making her way to the rose garden. The scent of the flowers was overwhelming, causing her to catch her breath as she fought off more tears. She paused, looking up at the pathway into the woods. Placing one foot in front of the other, she walked to the path and soon reached the gate to the sugar shack. The chain and padlock were hanging loose as if she was expected. In a dream-like state, Carla pushed open the gate and walked through. She half expected to see elves, fairies or other mystical creatures. With a slight laugh, she went on to the door of the little building. It too, was open. She stepped inside, and in a croak asked, "Is anyone here?" There was no answer. She looked around at the room and was only a little surprised to find it clean and orderly. Lester and Sam always took good care of the outbuildings. She slowly, as if in a dream, walked to the furnace room. As if she was supposed to be here, the furnace had a small fire burning in it. "Why?" She thought, her mind suddenly filling with panic. "What would he be doing out here?"

"Miss Carla?" Lester said from behind her.

Carla whirled around to face him. "There's a fire in the furnace," she said in a half whisper.

"Yes," he nodded. "I been burning tree limbs and such-like."

Carla stood, staring, not knowing what to say. Lester said something reasonable, but she had been expecting it to be horrible. *Is this what it's like to lose your mind? Is this what went on in Auntie Em's mind all the time?*

"What can I do for you?" He asked, removing his hat and twirling it around in his hands.

"I want to burn this," she said, shoving the diary at him.

Lester tried to take it from her, but she didn't let go. He dropped his hands to his sides and waited. Finally, after what seemed like a very long time, he spoke. "Do you want to just throw it into the furnace yourself, then?" He nodded at the open furnace now behind her.

Carla dropped the book on the floor and fled, sobbing and flailing her hands before her. She didn't stop until she reached the safety of her room upstairs. There, she stood once again with her back to the door, facing her window. Woodenly, she walked to the window and looked down on the garden where the roses looked beautiful, causing tears to stream down her face. Lester waved at her from the tractor as he drove toward the barn. "I wonder what he does out there......" she said aloud. The words echoed in the room. It was a twist on a familiar phrase.

THE END

Printed in the United States
by Baker & Taylor Publisher Services